DROP ZONE

Sever Squad

Book 1

A.R. KNIGHT

ONE

The Commander

HE CALLED her the wrong name. Twice. So Aurora whipped her hand back, and sent it crashing against the lunkhead's face. Skin rippled like an earthquake from where her palm bit into his cheek. His eyes flew up and his mouth screwed into a jagged line, as though all of the nerves in his head couldn't comprehend what had just happened. Then he dropped to the ground. Hit the floor like a bomb. One that sent the mess into deafening quiet.

"My name's Aurora. Get it right." She said, even though the man, from his glassed gaze, definitely wouldn't remember this.

Aurora cast the same threat around the hall. Bunch of rookies. New recruits to DefenseCorp. Staring back at her like she was a Gnarler, all tentacles and teeth. They were scared. As well they should be.

Aurora looked at them, elbows on the steel tables. Trays full of nutrient soup. The rookies were all shades, all types. Even a few E.T.'s in the mix. A trio of willowy Casparians, their thin membranes making them almost translucent.

DefenseCorp must be expanding its horizons. Marketing to species that don't breed like rabbits, like humans. Convincing them that hard-earned cash and a big cannon were worth risking your life. Not the worst message.

It'd worked on her.

"You see what happened to this guy here?" Aurora announced to the silence. "He didn't respect his superior. He didn't respect me. And when you don't respect me, you don't respect who you work for. And if you don't respect DefenseCorp, this is what happens." She pointed at the body on the ground.

Another reason she liked working for DefenseCorp? This guy decorating the floor right here. None of that standard issue government regulation. Just good old-fashioned survival of the fittest. Fatter paychecks too.

Aurora resumed walking. Left the hall and the food that she didn't want behind. As fun as it was to strike some fear into the rookies, she'd only been going through the mess on her way to someplace more important: the bridge.

The Odin-class cruiser *Nautilus*. The home of nearly 200,000 people. Made from an asteroid's core, hollowed out, refined and sent off on journeys to the most dangerous, most profitable parts of the galaxy DefenseCorp could find. Anywhere chaos planted its seeds, DefenseCorp showed up ready to kill and clear, for the right price. The company the galaxy paid to handle blood work, clean up the aftermath.

Aurora glanced at her wristlet as she walked—an easy motion, as it was bolted to her left wrist. Embedded, if you wanted to call it that. That way they couldn't be lost. That way the batteries, if necessary, could recharge off her own body heat. Aurora kept it running in low power mode no matter how long she was out. Until she died, anyway.

The wristlet blinked an orange alert at her. As it had been the last ten minutes. The time it'd taken Aurora to go from her quarters, through the mess hall, knock out the lunkhead, and now to get here.

The *Nautilus*'s bridge was larger than most stadiums. A huge space, for a huge amount of officers. Scanners, computers, giant domes for people to sit in that would provide 3-D modeling of everything going on. Right now, though, the *Nautilus* was in transit. Which meant the view out the ship's front was all black, starry sparkles washed out by the blue-white interior lights. Off on the right, a pinkish nebula glowed. Pretty, if you had the time for that sort of thing.

"Took you long enough," Commander Deepak said. The man stood tall. Rippling in a skin suit that he never took off. That all DefenseCorp commanders had to wear as part of their rank. Seeing it made Aurora's standard-issue cloth itch.

A skin suit provided the usual comforts. Regulated Deepak's body temp, killed poisons that made their way into his bloodstream, and happened to look just like a snazzy crimson uniform. The collar brushed up to the bottom of Deepak's chin, a dark one covered with not a micrometer of hair.

"I tried to run, but someone got in my way." Aurora didn't bother shrugging. Deepak knew any obstacle had been removed.

"It's fine," Deepak said. "I called you because twenty minutes ago we received a covert SOS. VIP customer, so it's need to know. Your squad is being pulled from our main assignment to handle this one, and we're almost to the drop point. You have your squad ready?"

"I read the message," Aurora said. "Sever will be set to launch on time."

"And you?" Deepak replied. "You're good on the particulars?"

"It's a standard for Sever, right?" Aurora said. "Get in, raise all manner of bloody hell, then get out?"

"With the client, yes," Deepak smiled. "One warning though—you won't be getting an extraction. We can't delay our primary contract."

No extract? That didn't sound right. On occasion, Sever would do a drop and run. But that just meant the extraction would be delayed. Sever would hold their own, wait undercover after completing the mission and eventually some shuttle or another would show up and give them a ride back home. Deepak wasn't talking about that though. She could tell in his voice, which held a final note to it.

"What do you mean?" Aurora almost added *sir*, but this wasn't the military. You didn't have to call your commanding officers titles. They weren't even really officers. Just bosses.

"It means you have to find your own way off world," Deepak said. "This contract is strictly classified. We can't have evidence that DefenseCorp was involved."

"Won't it be pretty evident? My squad doesn't operate in the dark."

"You the best, Aurora. That's why you're getting this assignment. You and Sever will figure it out. Buy a shuttle, or steal one. You'll be reimbursed."

And if they couldn't?

Aurora didn't ask the question, because she knew the answer.

TWO

Demolition Man

THE PROBLEM with simulations were that the bombs didn't feel real. Sai sat back on the cot. Stared at his cabin's wall, a black glass slate doubling as his computer screen, at the stats pouring out. The chemical mixture Sai came up with didn't quite reach the temp needed to cut through hard steel. And if the detonation couldn't do that, then the whole idea was worthless. He raised his fist, ready to pound down on his desk, and stopped. Come on. Hitting things never solved the problem.

Well, not computer problems.

His cabin was one half cot, one quarter locker, and one quarter screen. His bed brushed right up against the glow. Sai fell back on the mattress. Hard, scratchy blankets. A pillow. When those didn't work, a little gas vent hooked up to the side wall. People had trouble sleeping on a ship this size, with this much noise. A couple deep breaths of the good stuff and Sai would cash out till his room's alarm, tied into his bed, shocked him awake at the right time. The gas tended to kill the nightmares too, a plus given how often Sever's old missions replayed themselves in his dreams. Didn't need to see most of those again. Ever.

Sai would've taken a hit right then and there, except his wristlet computer started blinking. A green light. No incoming message, then, but an order. More exciting than sleep, at least.

Sai curled up and twisted on his cot, slipped his legs off the side and pressed open his locker with a palm to the door. The thin, crimson-painted door slid open and revealed standard issue DefenseCorp armor. Ridged, plated metal made up the suit's core. Awkward, but the plates protected Sai from just about anything. Built-in heat dispersion to send the hot energy from a laser spreading around his body and then out the back. Effective enough that the only stuff that could really hurt Sai were concentrated beams, or close-up knives. Things that could get in between those plates.

The armor compensated for its weight with boosters locked into the feet, legs, back and arms. Every motion Sai made would get an extra lift from the suit's gears, making Sai something of a super soldier, albeit one that could be quickly rendered useless if his tech shorted out. Also, the damn things really stank once you'd spent more than a few hours in one.

But that blinking green light didn't give him a choice. Anytime he saw that, it meant go and go hard.

Sai reached out with his arms and put one hand in each of the suit's gloves. The armor felt the gesture and jumped forward out of the locker towards him. The first three times Sai had done this, he'd fallen back on the cot, with the armor collapsing on him. Not dignified, and definitely uncomfortable. Eventually, he'd figured out how to brace his legs, to attach the armor's various pieces to make sure he didn't overbalance. The same way he learned to fire a gun. The same way he stopped being scared.

Repetition made the unusual usual.

The metal slats ran across his arms and legs. The suit fit to his torso and before Sai had a chance to take a breath, the helmet slid over his head. The visor dropped over his eyes and lit up. The armor jacked into his wristlet and, just like that, his whole body became one with the galaxy's most expensive assault gear.

An overlay appeared on the visor across his eyes. Quick readouts on system operations. The suit's condition, his oxygen level, temp, blood pressure.

One other thing popped up too. What Sai always looked for first. Five out of five. His squad all punching up and getting in. That meant it hadn't been a mistake. Sever Squad had received an order.

Go time.

Before he left his quarters, Sai turned, a bulky ask in the armor, and a move that nearly had him falling over onto his own bed. He leaned over and wiped away, with a gesture, the bomb data. Then stared, briefly, at what filled the screen. A video. A direct feed to his wife, his son and daughter. Obviously not live—that kind of data took a long time to cross these light years—but Sai kept it streaming the last bit until new footage came in. It would rewind to the beginning if Sai had nothing new to see.

The three of them were eating in the kitchen this time. A real breakfast, not the vitamin mush DefenseCorp fed them here. Around a circular white stone table—Maria had bought that with Sai's last DefenseCorp bonus—in a house that had no glass windows. Open-air jungle letting the planet's yellow star peek in from outside. Peaceful, calm. Normal. Sai had never seen it, and yet he lived there every minute he spent in this room.

The video fluttered, reset to the beginning. Then Sai wiped that too.

THREE

Hammer Time

IT NEVER GOT OLD; clomping down the hall and watching all the rookies and people who didn't know better jump out of his way. Every stomp made Gregor feel like a behemoth, a wrecking ball. Power's benefits never had clearer evidence.

Gregor eyed the panels on either side as he moved; static metal when nobody came by, but as soon as there was motion, the panels would flip on. Meet them with your eyes and they would show your current orders. The fastest route to your destination. Anything else that you could imagine. It's why people lingered in the hallways when they were bored. You could see what else there was to do. Where you needed to be.

Which meant Gregor had targets. As he went, clad in his mottled green-gray suit, he pantomimed blasting away everyone he passed. Occasionally took a swipe, though never quite connecting. Everyone either screamed, ducked, or dove out of the way.

"Gregor, pull yourself together," Aurora's voice came over his armor's comm array. "I'm trying to get my suit on and my comm's blowing up with complaints. I don't have time for this crap."

"Got to keep my reputation," Gregor replied.

The passage through the *Nautilus* from Sever's quarters to their assigned docking bay was short. Five minutes or less transition time. Intentional. So when Gregor arrived, the sliding doors in the bay scanning him through a red eye at the gate's top, he paused for a moment, surprised he was first. Inside the bay sat their drop shuttle. Gregor saw the boarding ramp already down and realized he was wrong. There in the cockpit, relaxed and staring straight at nothing, sat Eponi in her rose-red suit. Figured she'd be here.

Eponi practically lived in that thing.

Which, Gregor realized, he'd probably live in it too if he could. They wouldn't trust him with something like the shuttle though. Too many weapons. Be too easy to forget to fly with so many things to play with. Most DefenseCorp missions were what Deepak, their boss, called "target-rich environments". With all the blasting, Gregor wouldn't even notice someone on his tail.

Without even thinking about it, he reached behind his back. Felt the cold metal handle of his passion. The hammer stretched over a meter long. More than capable, with its round head, of bashing in steel doors. Plus, it packed a motion-activated battery that, after a few swings, could add enough oomph to knock you to the stratosphere.

Someone bumped him, squeezing by.

"You ever try being polite?" Gregor said. The new kid was in his ocean-blue suit. Small, quirky. The kind of thing that wouldn't scare a fly.

"You ever learn to move?" The kid replied.

Rovo, that was the rookie's name. Gregor had already forgotten who the kid replaced. Bodies came and went. If you made it through a few missions, then maybe Gregor would care enough to get to know you. Maybe.

"Only for people that deserve it," Gregor replied.

"Get in that shuttle, or you'll deserve a lot worse," Aurora's voice came from behind them.

Gregor turned and saw she wasn't really looking his way. She had her eyes scrolling the info on her visor like always. Monitoring the squad's progress. Her peppered black and white suit sparkled. All their armor started clean and gleaming, ended gross and riddled with burn marks. Gregor knew which he preferred.

Seeing the kid and Aurora standing there, not even watching him, made Gregor twitch. It wasn't like Gregor wanted to throttle his commander right there. It wasn't like he wanted to squash Rovo. But at the same time, Gregor's bones were ready. Once he got himself good and juiced, he needed to get to whacking, or else it would all be wasted.

"We dropping soon?" Gregor said.

Aurora looked up at him. "Like I said. You get on that shuttle, and we'll go."

Gregor shrugged. Fine. He turned and climbed up the ramp that led to the crowded interior. Hard gray seats, crash netting and harnesses. Labels plastered around detailing emergency procedures, though everyone knew if you had an emergency in a shuttle like this one, you were probably dead. At least each seat had a lever next to it that, if pulled down, would cut the netting's connections so they could get out in a flash. Make one last glorious dive into the sky if this shuttle was going down.

Gregor had only pulled it three times. Twice it was even necessary.

He took a seat, clipped himself in. Stared at the countdown clock. Three minutes. A hundred and eighty seconds to grind his teeth and wait.

FOUR

Stick Jockey

SHE HIT the switch break hard, shifting the splash kart to the right and around the large sandstone rock in the course's center. The stone was a new one, an obstacle the owners must've placed after last year's zero fatality race.

It almost caught Eponi by surprise. And, going by the fiery cloud in her rear-view, someone else didn't make it.

She still had two racers ahead, their splash karts cutting over the water as each played the wind and waves for advantage, their microjets keeping them just above the surf.

No chance for Eponi to catch up.

Not if she played by the rules.

A floating barge, covered with the audience, loomed. A dome over the top played video feeds of the race from aerial drones, which kept the sides of the barge clear for actual viewing. Most would be cheering, drinking, partying —the race an afterthought.

The course, lined by glowing buoys on either side, split around the barge. At least, the visible part did. Eponi killed her microjets, and her kart dove into the water. The glass cockpit kept her dry as she plunged beneath the surface. Eponi shunted the energy to her rear fan to counter the water's resistance, sped up and shot along the undercurrent beneath the floating barge. Before she cleared it, Eponi triggered the microjets back on again. Rocketed to the surface and shot up into the air just on the other side. The two racers ahead of her now barely behind.

Eponi couldn't hear the cheers, but she was sure she'd earned them. As for the other two karts, they'd run out of course to race. The blaze-orange buoys that marked the finish were right—

"Eponi?"

The vision blurred. Then her helmet's video faded and revealed the drop shuttle's transparent windshield and, beyond, the *Nautilus*'s static outer hull. No race. No cheers.

Only memories.

"Thinking of something else?" Rovo said. The little guy climbed to the cockpit next her. A two-seater. Aurora would normally take front with Eponi here, but in an unknown sector? You needed somebody who could talk no matter who picked up, even if they were a rookie.

"Better days," Eponi replied.

"Really? You didn't know me then." Rovo's voice was deeper than you'd think for a man his size. Scratchy. Maybe he'd spent too much time in smoke-filled rooms, maybe that was where he'd learned to talk all those tongues.

"Believe me, life was just fine before you came in it," Eponi said.

But Rovo was right. No time for memories. Not with the rest of the squad on board. Or almost—Eponi saw Sai stumble into the bay. The man was always late. Like her, obsessing over other things. Unlike her, Sai kept his memories in his room rather than where he needed to be. Amateur.

The second Sai's foot hit the ramp, Eponi pressed the button to retract it. Made Sai scamper up the steps. Might teach him a lesson. At least it made her laugh.

"You could hurt him, doing that." Rovo actually sounded worried. Like he cared.

The rookie's sentiment was cute, but it would die soon enough.

"He gets hurt getting on the shuttle, that's his own fault," Eponi replied. "I'm the one that gets blamed if we lift off late." Time for a topic switch, get the rookie focused on more important things. "You know anything about where we're going?"

The deflect worked—Rovo's eyes went all out of focus. That look he had when he was trying to remember something.

"The same as you." He said finally. "Nothing."

"A world called Dynas," Aurora said as she entered the cockpit. She stood behind the two of them, putting her gloved hands on the backs of the chairs. "A wet, mossy place. A lot of natural resources. Interesting wildlife. We're doing a search and rescue, then extract."

"Only we don't have an extraction," Eponi said. The briefing had said that much.

"We'll just have to play it smart," Aurora said. "Not burn out our drop shuttle for once."

"That never works, and you know it."

There's a reason why drop shuttles had the name. Designed to get a squad down, giving covering fire, and act as a base until you'd done what you needed to do. Most times they couldn't get back up. Most times they weren't meant to.

"Sounds like you're doubting us," Aurora said. "Don't have room for doubt on the squad."

"I don't have any doubt," Eponi said. "I'm just being real, commander."

"Well, in that case, stop being real and start getting us out of here." Aurora turned and walked back to where the harness awaited her.

Eponi radioed the bridge. Received the clear and activated, with a press on the center console, the departure sequence. Behind them, big metal doors slid open. At the same time, in front of her, the door leading out of the docking bay and back into the *Nautilus* closed. Then a secondary barrier slammed down over it. No chance of vacuum. No chance of something going wrong.

As the doors revealed dark space, Eponi could see, through the shuttle's rear cameras and framed around the edges, *Nautilus*'s rocky exterior. The remnants of the asteroid. While ship's frame sat inside the rock, the bulky exterior had been left. The shell provided good armor. Even some first-look camouflage.

The drop shuttle's engines started with a soft hum, the battery draining to spin them up. They'd superheat a tank of fuel—a limited supply, yet another reason why drop shuttles weren't meant to survive, and thrust the ship forward. Beneath the shuttle, on its underside, four microjets burst to life. Bigger than those on the karts, and capable of bouncing the shuttle up a meter.

Eponi slipped a black and green glove over the armor on her left hand and felt the tingle as tiny nodes in the fabric signaled a connection with the computer in her wrist. She raised the hand, careful to keep her fingers bent, until she reached eye level.

Rovo kept quiet. Smart man.

When Eponi straightened her fingers, laying her hand

flat in the air, the glove flashed red and stayed that color. Ready to fly. Eponi moved her hand to the right, keeping it level, and the shuttle started a slow turn. She held her hand steady until the shuttle faced outer space, a complete 180 degree twist. Then, with her right hand, she pushed forward on the throttle, kicking the shuttle out.

She'd marveled when DefenseCorp first gave Eponi a look at the technology. Virtual pilot. No need to grab the flight stick, no need to panic if a wire snapped or the stick stuck, or if Eponi was thrown away and suddenly unable to grab it. Now, so long as Eponi wore the glove, it would interlace with the shuttle, and let her hand control the ship alone.

If she wanted to, Eponi could leave the cockpit. Could go all the way outside and still fly the shuttle. If she had this glove on, the ship would be like putty in her hands.

They flew out of the *Nautilus*, into the black void of space. Black except for a green dot, one steadily getting larger. They still had all the momentum of the *Nautilus* going at full speed. Though now that they were moving perpendicular, the cruiser quickly shrank in size. Even a massive thing like that disappeared fast when they were moving at thousands of kilometers an hour. Deepak had been kind enough to slow the big ship as much as he could, and now most of Eponi's fuel would be spent bringing the drop shuttle down to a velocity that could handle atmosphere without blowing into a billion pieces.

"Dynas," Rovo said. "Never heard of this planet."

"If you haven't heard of it, then I sure as hell haven't," Eponi replied. Not necessarily true, but if a world wasn't on the racing circuit, Eponi didn't need to know it existed. Not till now anyway.

In front of her, at knee level, the center console changed. A map of the region on Dynas where they were supposed to go. Possible landing zones showed up in yellow. Not more than a few kilometers away from each other, which meant a defined objective. At least the area was tight. She hated being given a continent to choose from.

"A secret VIP?" Eponi said. "Who do you think this guy is? Some rich investor? A politician?"

"If I don't know a planet, it's because it's a backwater. It's because nobody does," Rovo said. "Which means if we're going there, on this short notice, someone's really screwed up. And, for DefenseCorp to care, really rich."

FIVE

The Diplomat

THERE WERE TOO MANY WORDS. And when you count all the languages, that just multiplied the number. Which meant Rovo had a lot of learning to do.

He tried, too. Even right there, sitting by Eponi in the cockpit, behind his visor's lens, Rovo poured over the next one: Casparian. More a series of tones and inflections than actual words. Once you figured out how to curl your tongue *just so*, it wasn't that hard to figure out. Amazing, really, what that species could do with sound. Humanity, with its giant mess of dialects—even if Common had trampled all the other languages by now—could learn a thing or two.

But then again, maybe he ought to be paying attention. Eponi was saying something. When Rovo blinked away his lens overlay, he saw a blue cast had taken over his console. Incoming transmission. Outside the front viewport, what had been Dynas's green dot had grown huge. Filled most of the windshield now.

"Hey, you can answer that?" Eponi was saying.

"Maybe. What if I don't?" Rovo replied.

"I'll kick your ass. Then Aurora will do it, and then Gregor will finish you up."

Rovo knew Eponi couldn't see his face, but he screwed it up anyway. The thought of Gregor laying into him? No thank you. So he pressed the console. Stared at the strange face suddenly looking back at him.

It was human, definitely. But not only that. The man was splotched with greens and blacks, as if he'd been injected with mold. Wrapped up and left to rot for a while. Then taken out, steamed and oiled up. Not an appealing picture.

"We read your approach," the man said, his voice watery, like he had a bad cold. "What's your purpose on Dynas?"

"Just stopping by," Rovo said. "Wanted to see the sights."

There were some planets, ones with city centers, with grand natural wonders. There you could pretend to be a tourist. You could show some real, honest to goodness affection for the planet and land without a lot of hassle. A place like Dynas? Rovo checked the scanners, no visible ship traffic. Dynas was a place you went for a reason, and Sever didn't have a good one.

"What sites are you talking about?" The man said.

"Well, what sites do you have?" Rovo replied. He had one responsibility right now: keep the people talking. Keep them confused, off-balance. Then, once Eponi got the shuttle below any defenses, he could fling as many insults as he liked.

Really, it wasn't the worst job.

"I request that you turn around, and abandon your route."

"We don't have the fuel to do that," Rovo said. "You have a place we can touchdown? Recharge?"

Not that the drop shuttle could get enough power to actually fly them to another world. Beyond the engines, the shuttle operated on batteries, which could only be recharged given the right infrastructure. A thing Rovo didn't believe Dynas had, going by the looks of it.

On the consoles, readings sprang up as the drop shuttle sensors pressed out. Spikes of energy, heat. Those overlays appeared on the front viewport. And they were few. What-ever settlements Dynas had, they were small, or very well disguised.

"Your problems are not our problems. Turn around, or we will defend ourselves."

"Doesn't seem like you and I are getting along. You have a manager? Someone else I can talk to?" Rovo said. He muted his side of the call, pressed the suit's transponder—already patched into the squads short-wave frequency. "Hey guys, get ready. Looks like a rocky entrance."

"We always have rocky entrances," Eponi said.

"Don't lie," Rovo said, after he'd released the transpon-der. "You like 'em."

Eponi didn't say anything, but Rovo would've bet everything he had she was smiling under that armor.

Dynas and its foggy green filled everything they could see. The shuttle began to shake as it hit atmosphere and the heavy air in it. Rovo grabbed handles, then realized he hadn't actually closed the call. On the other side, the strange looking man yelled at them, his splotched mouth opening, closing, and his face red. If anything, it looked even more disgusting than before.

Rovo touched the screen one more time. Figured there'd be an opportunity to score one last insult.

"You're all going to die. Do you hear me? Every last one of you." The man cut the call.

Rovo didn't even get in his shot. He'd have to deliver it in person.

SIX

Wet Landing

_____

Aurora heard Rovo's warning call and responded with habit, "Set'em up and let'em loose."

Three Severs sat in the back in crash harnesses and each pressed a small button under their right hand. The shuttle's ceiling held drop-down screens hanging from metal bars. The displays swung right in front of the Sever's faces, each perfectly aligned thanks to micro-cameras measuring eye level. Each screen flipped to show a cannon's feed. Two on the bottom—split to the bow and aft of the shuttle—and one on top, all charged and ready to fire.

Aurora's snapped on first, giving her the front-facing lower cannon. Showed the world of stormy, musty yellow-gray fog they were descending into as the shuttle went lower and lower. Nothing appeared on her scopes. Who knew whether Dynas had any kind of defense, but survival dictated acting as if the planet bristled with death.

"I'm picking up a heat signature, looks like energy use," Eponi said through their transponders. "Gonna land on top of it. Feel it's as good a spot as any."

"Just don't get us killed," Sai said.

"Do I ever?"

"Any sign of threats?" Aurora snapped. She had no problem with squad banter, so long as it didn't distract in a dangerous moment.

"No," Eponi replied, but her voice trailed even as she spoke. "Wait—coming behind. A pair of Darter-class skiffs."

Skiffs? If they flew open top craft like those here, then Dynas had a thick atmosphere. Breathable. Skiffs also meant Dynas didn't understand who they were dealing with. Sure, not having a plated hull or windshield might make for pretty views, but it also made for an easy target. Couldn't shield open space. Aurora would have loved to trigger a few shots and let go the tight knots that always formed in her muscles as missions began, but Gregor had the rear cannon, and the first chance to speckle Dynas's fog with the enemy's bits and pieces.

The drop ship didn't shudder when Gregor fired his cannon, a total lack of feedback Aurora should have been used to by now. No projectiles, like in the old models, so no recoil. Just a hum. A draining battery's whine.

As battle went, lasers made the whole thing feel artificial, like they were playing a game. Aurora knew that feeling would vanish with the first casualty showing what a laser's direct strike could do to a person, but Gregor's fire didn't deliver that absolution.

"They're splitting their approach. Lightly armed," Gregor said after his initial volley. "I see two cannons on each one, mounted bow and aft. I've already neutralized the front cannon on mine."

"Only because your pilot doesn't know how to dodge," Sai added. "Mine at least understands the concept."

The soupy fog broke as Eponi soared the shuttle down.

Lush deep green poked through, caught by the drop shuttle's lights, which Eponi switched on as the clouds, now above, consumed most starlight daring to try and get this far. If Aurora had to guess, the reason Dynas had life at all came down to its heat trap of an atmosphere boiling up biologic sludge from whatever unlucky rock collection collided to form Dynas in the first place.

"Keep your eyes open for ground defenses," Eponi said.

The shuttle rattled as Eponi finished. Something popped and smoke flooded into the cabin. No, not smoke. Fog from outside.

"What was that?" Aurora snapped.

"The skiffs." Sai replied. "Not the main cannons. Something weird. From handheld rifles. My guess, homing drones with explosives attached. Can we move any faster?"

"This is a drop shuttle, Sai. We're basically falling." The cocky sass vanished from Eponi's voice, signaling a pilot focusing on her flying.

Which meant a serious situation. Aurora cut off her own urge to ask Eponi for details—one of the hardest parts about leading Sever lay in trusting the team, holding off the urge to question their every action, ask for and approve of every detail.

"The second skiff is cutting overhead!" Gregor yelled.

Aurora didn't need to hear anymore. Her view screen flashed bright yellow in the upper left corner; the shuttle's scanners indicating a target. Aurora used her eyes, dragging them to the target's position. The move aimed the cannon, and she stared back up into that fog. Waited. The contact between Aurora's eyes and the screen kept the feed active, the cannon primed.

A long dark shadow cut across the screen. Aurora blinked both eyes and the cannon fired a bright green bolt into the ether. Aurora blinked again and again and again, sending shots towards the shape, which flared into a beautiful orange and red rose.

Skiff down.

"Took care of it," Aurora said.

But the fog kept flowing into the drop shuttle. Aurora couldn't see the hole, and unstrapping during a potential crash landing scenario would put Aurora on the wrong side of every DefenseCorp guide. And common sense—the drop shuttle still continued doing what it had been made for: dropping. The ship wouldn't have to hold up for much longer.

"Sorry, Sever, seems like that shot killed my coolant. Engines are overheating. Going down here because, uh, otherwise we're all getting cooked." Eponi said. "Brace for a wet landing."

Aurora aimed her cannon down in time to see massive branches, trees, and vines snag the shuttle and swallow it up. The cannon feed held, then shook and went dark. The shuttle filled with roaring, wrecking, tearing as Sever rattled in their seats. Seats that didn't break, because DefenseCorp bolted every drop shuttle chair to the floor with heavy metals. Meant to handle an impact, and to stop a sharp object from piercing through the floor and hurting its occupant.

Aurora had been in plenty of crashes, a standard hazard in this line of work, but most had been on land. One on a beach, as part of a rescue in a resort overtaken by discontent alien tourists. But none into a swamp. So when the shuttle smacked into the water, bounced forward, and settled into a noxious mix of slimy water and terrible gasses, Aurora had a new candidate for worst place ever. She unclipped, clocked the power readings on her armor —all greens—and made for the shuttle's opening sides.

Swamp water had the same idea, flooding into the ship to greet Aurora with frothy filth.

"Pop out!" Aurora said the words that nobody needed to hear. Gregor and Sai, following her, scrambled through the open door in the left hull, made larger courtesy of a now-downed tree that'd taken its final stab through the drop shuttle's side.

Eponi and Rovo had already evacuated, having climbed out through the shattered cockpit window. Rovo looked towards the sky, hunting for any further skiffs, while Eponi leaned back into the cockpit, swatting at buttons. Protocol said it'd be best to shut down the drop shuttle's systems, drain the batteries in the event of a harsh landing to prevent bad things like enemy scavenging and random explosions.

"What happened?" Aurora yelled to Eponi when the pilot settled back on the drop ship's nose. "You didn't make the hit sound serious?"

"Whatever they fired at us?" Eponi shot back. "It kept going. I lost systems one by one. Had to take us down fast or we would have run right through these trees."

Aurora looked out over the desolate swamp stretching as far as she could see, which, given the dark, misty conditions, wasn't all that far. Their attackers, whomever lived on Dynas, weren't looking for visitors. They were ready to kill to keep their world quiet, but they'd missed their chance.

Sever wouldn't give them a second one.

SEVEN

Swamp Thing

A SEWER. That's what this planet felt like, and Sai had only been on it for a minute. The fog seeped down in great green-gray sheets, a sticky mist coating his armor, clogging the breathing vents, and sending its rotting odor into Sai's nose. The filters would kick out anything harmful, but smells could stay. Sai would like to punch whatever engineer probably declared, smug degrees running through their voice, that keeping scents could be useful. Could be a warning.

Sai wouldn't be any good if he kept coughing like this.

Gregor put his armored fist against Sai's back as the two of them stood on the drop shuttle's side. If Sai didn't take a step soon, Gregor's weight said, the big man would push Sai into the swamp. Dynas didn't have crushing gravity, but Sai's weight, with the armor, would be enough here to drag him down to the depths. Where, naturally, the suit would let him breathe. But if things were this ugly up here, imagine what they'd be underneath the yellow-green glop?

"I'm moving," Sai said, keeping his voice on the squad channel. "Settle down."

"I'm not excited," Gregor replied. "We are vulnerable up here."

If the skiffs could see them through the fog, they'd already be dead, but Sai didn't argue. Instead, he took the first step down. Off the shuttle and onto what looked like a muddy rock. His foot hit the material, and sank right down through. The metal boot descended, and his leg followed up to his knee before Sai hit something not quite solid, but thick enough to support his weight.

"Careful," Sai said. "The ground likes to eat people."

The others followed, though Sai noticed they stuck to walking on the shuttle itself. Kept to its fins and floating hull. He felt their eyes on him. Waiting to see if he disappeared. If he became a casualty, a statistic.

Jerks, the lot of them.

He heard Aurora start talking to Eponi, and decided to take a second step, leaving the shuttle entirely and clomping in the goop. Then a third, though the mud sucked at his legs, forcing a yanking, squelching cadence.

His respirators confirmed the breathable atmosphere, five times thicker than Earth's. Humid and drenched. So much so that if they stayed on the surface too long, their suits would rust over.

"Sai, what are you doing?" Aurora sounded like a taut ripcord, one tug away from losing it. "Do you know where you're going?"

"Standard protocol," Sai replied. "Get away from a crashed ship after landing."

"As you may have noticed, this isn't standard," Aurora said, then seemed to check herself. "But Sai does have a point. Eponi, you know where we should go? Where's the station you were heading for?"

Eponi, standing on the nose of the shuttle, pointed off to the distance, to Sai's left. From what Sai could tell, insofar as the suit's compass told him, Eponi's heading went north.

A working compass was a miracle—whether Defense-Corp skimped out on them or Sever managed to dodge planets with magnetic polarity, the little red and white arrows proved more useless than not on their missions. Here, with visibility maybe ten meters, any distant navigation would be done by non-visual methods. Regardless, the chosen direction didn't match where Sai had been trudging.

Sai twisted, swung his legs through the muck. Took a step forward. His left leg lurched. Slid back. Something grabbed his foot. A steady pull, no yanks. Drawing Sai deeper into the muck.

"Something's got me!" Sai yelped. He twisted, but the only thing he could see was that damn mist, the burbling, slimy mud.

His left hand fumbled for the laser pistol on his hip. Grabbed it, swung around, and almost pulled the trigger. DefenseCorp standard regs said not to fire without a clear visual of the target—collateral damage cost cash, and came out of Sever's paycheck.

Sai's right hand tapped his helmet, pressing against his temple, and the visor flipped from standard to infrared. The mustard greens faded to blackish-blue, except for his own heat, and that of the creature coming after him. The thing had wrapped itself around his foot, large and roiling.

Sai may have screamed.

"Gregor," Aurora answered Sai's panic with a solution. If Sai had to pick one trait about the commander that explained why Aurora held the position, it would be this one: when the tight cord keeping her control snapped, she became razor ice, cold and ruthless. "Jump in."

"Yes." Gregor, in his black and silver suit, reached over

his head and grabbed his hammer. Pulled it over, readied it in both hands.

"Wait!" Sai started, hoping for a chance to get away from impending disaster, but one could sooner stop a comet than halt Gregor's assault.

The monstrous man crouched and jumped. All suits came with push pads in their boot soles. If needed, they could supply a microburst of downward force by sucking power from the armor's motion-charged batteries. Add two to three extra meters on a jump or more with momentum.

The boost gave Gregor the height to come crashing down beyond Sai, leading with his hammer. Gregor drove the weapon through the mud, followed by its owner. Sai couldn't tell what happened, because a wall of muck slammed over him.

Mad laughter filled the comm.

Sai flipped back to standard vision, wiped away the dreck and stared at his armor. Once emerald green, Sai now had perfect, foul-smelling camouflage. No metal in sight.

Not that Sai had much time to think about his coming cleaning nightmare. Rovo and Aurora announced their arrival to the fight with yellow laser blasts scorching the slime in front of Sai, the thing Gregor had swatted with his hammer rose up from the waters.

A thing that kept rising. Until it stood more than three times higher than Sai himself. It seemed unfair for something that ugly to be that tall. As if mud had suddenly achieved life, and brought along the gunk, sticks and stones to sentience with it. Pieces broke and drifted off the creature, splashing into the swamp water around Sax.

"It's got tentacles," Rovo said, splashing in next to Sai. "Because of course it does."

Gray and mottled, coated with spots of mold, the

tentacles shivered as the thing grew out of the swamp. They draped along the thing's sides, and Sai counted at least ten, possibly more, with the ends vanishing beneath the surface. Sai looked for a mouth. For eyes. Found none.

This monster was a giant blob, one seemingly intent on turning Sever Squad into its next meal.

EIGHT

Tentacle Time

GREGOR LAUGHED. Shook his head at the sight of the creature, and then laughed some more. He didn't expect to find this kind of entertainment out here, so far away from any active combat zones, on some long DefenseCorp patrol given to Sever and the *Nautilus* as a sort-of break. And here he was, face to face with something he'd never seen, never heard of.

The monster was disgusting. A living mess.

And very smashable.

His visor, coated with a super-slick film, washed off the mud that stuck to every other part of him. Gregor had to heft twice to pull his hammer out of the grime it'd been stuck in after his swing. Fine. He preferred having to work for his fun.

Holding his maul in his hands, Gregor stared up at the blob. Looked for a weak point. Didn't find any, which meant straight ahead.

"Cleared to go in?" Gregor said.

"Cleared," Aurora replied a moment later, her voice coming clean through their suit's communications.

They gave Gregor a break in their laser fire. Sever's assault weapons would superheat a mud beast like this one and turn it into a boiling mass of crap. Before that happened, Gregor wanted to get his swings in. He double pumped his heels, activating the boost pads in his boots, and Gregor popped out of the mud. He swung the hammer left to right as Gregor flew through the air and connected with the mud beast.

Grime and glory splattered all over as the weapon found its mark. Then the hammer head stuck, and Gregor, his momentum still going, flew chest first into the front of the beast. Smacked it like a wet noodle, the hit jarring Gregor's weapon free—of his grip, the mud still had strong hold of the hammer—and Gregor rolled down the thing's front, splashing in the water at its base.

On his back, he could see his hammer still sticking out of the creature as Sever's bright yellow bolts resumed. He had to get the hammer back. Couldn't risk losing it in the swamp. Gregor tried to sit up when something collided with his face. Pressed him back down into the muck and cut off his vision.

"Gregor, hold on! One of the tentacles—" Sai, the one who got them into this mess, shouted.

"I can tell," Gregor cut him off. "Get it off me."

Gregor's suit registered the ripples in the water as Sai made his way over, while Gregor reached with his hands and grabbed the tentacle slamming his face down into the swamp. Tried to get a good grip, but the slime-coated trunk made for difficult grabbing from a pair of metal-covered armored gloves. Far from the first time, Gregor cursed DefenseCore's suit design.

He'd have to find another way.

Fine.

Gregor dropped his left hand away to his waist, slapped

it against the side of his power suit and popped a small little disk free. Held it up into the air, just out of the water, and squeezed. A single long blade unfurled from the center of the disk, and once it had straightened, the last quarter of it bent to a right angle, blade to the side. Gregor couldn't see any of this, but felt the expected vibrations in his hand as the tool spun up. An emergency saw.

Gregor held the blade to the trunk. Felt it dig into the muddy, moldy mass. And just as quickly felt the blade gum up. Snap and break apart. Not surprising—the disks were meant to cut through malfunctioning harnesses, safety nets, and ropes. Not cleave through a mud monster in the swamps of Dynas.

Gregor felt, rather than saw, Sai collide with the trunk. A shuddering charge, which did nothing. At least that Gregor could tell.

"Your sword, Sai," Gregor yelled.

That was Sai's whole point anyway. Bombs and blades.

"I wanted to keep it clean," Sai replied. Because of course he did.

"The creature will appreciate that after it's killed you."

The pressure increased, and the tentacle pushed Gregor further beneath the water's surface. Till he felt the swamp-floor mud sucking at his back. Creasing into his armor and wrapping around the sides of his helmet. He'd be buried in moments.

All once the pressure ceased. Gregor had his own power again. He pressed his arms, kicked his legs under him, and pushed them into the goop. Propelled his way to the surface. The suits weren't made for swimming, but the swamp wasn't an ocean, the shallow and thick water here gave Gregor enough heft to pull himself to the surface.

The end of the trunk still stuck to Gregor's mask, so he

couldn't see, but the little heads-up display, in neon blue letters, told him he'd made it out of the muck. That he could, if Gregor so chose, open his helmet without sending swamp water cascading in.

Opening a helmet in a live combat zone, unless in cases of critical malfunction, was against DefenseCorp policy. Voided his insurance—particularly the large payout that would come if Gregor met his demise. Too much to lose, and Gregor had heard DefenseCorp would take any opening it had to keep that payout low. Like most of Sever, family—parents, in his case—waited and no doubt hoped to one day receive the final payout from Gregor's suicidal career choice.

Gregor set his hands to the trunk again and, without the rest of the tentacle pressing it, managed to tear the suction away from his helmet and launch the limb away into the swamp. Gregor could see Dynas again, and once more the world left Gregor utterly unimpressed.

The fight was going about as well as he'd expected. Aurora, Eponi and Rovo were still launching spit-fire at the creature, which seemed unaffected. Its tentacles whirled around, and Gregor saw that some of the them were longer than the shuttle, blazing through the air like swinging tree trunks. The monster made Sever dive and roll around. Dodge the swinging limbs, keep from getting sucked in, captured, or beat down into the muck. Near him, Sai finally tried to go to work with the blade, but every cut came away with more mud and zero creature.

Gregor could help with that. He turned towards the monster, saw a tentacle start to swim through the swamp towards him. The mercenary squatted and snarled, "Come and get me you bloated bastard."

The long, slimy limb swept out of the swamp and

Gregor jumped, caught hold of it as the tentacle scooped up beneath him. It lifted Gregor up, higher than the creature itself, trying to fling him off. Exactly what Gregor hoped. As a trunk flew over the mud creature's head, Gregor let go, dropping and spinning through the air until he landed, with a sickening splat, right on the creature's head. Not that there really was a head, more like the top of a mound.

Gregor glanced left, down. The hammer stuck a meter beneath him, jammed into the side of the beast. Even if he could get to it, how would Gregor swing it before he wound up back in the swamp? One problem at a time. Gregor reached over his back, where, aside from the hammer, hung a pair of heavy assault rifles. Latched into the back of his power suit. Ready to go.

He popped one off, swung it over his shoulder as Gregor knelt on the beast. Pressed the nozzle down into the top of the mound. Pulled the trigger and held it.

A DefenseCorp heavy assault rifle spewed fifty bolts a second. Even without a laser's recoil, repeated fire superheated the mirrors in the barrel and tended to send accuracy plummeting. The weapon ought to scare the living hell out of anything Gregor shot as it filled the air with lethal fire. But the monster was as big as a house, and Gregor was right on top of it. Accuracy was not a question. Terror a secondary concern. Death mattered most, and at this range, the assault rifle delivered.

Bolts bubbled down into the creature, boiling deep holes that, in the moments before mud rushed to fill them, Gregor could see what looked like green-colored flesh. Good to know something lived beneath the gunk, that they weren't fighting the swamp itself. Real life could be taken, could be scared away or burned to a crisp.

"The fun part's beneath the mud!" Gregor shouted.

And then he was flying. Hit by a tentacle, soaring through the air. Gregor felt a crack in his back as he slammed into a tree and plummeted face first into the mud.

Down and out.

NINE

Shock Jock

THREE SHOTS. Count'em. And Aurora said Eponi didn't do enough when Sever started fights.

Not that those three shots—blistering bolts fired from the small rifle DefenseCorp regulations made Eponi carry —seemed to bother the swamp creature. Sever's pilot watched from the drop shuttle's front nose, the ship steadily losing its war against the loose sludge drawing it down, as Gregor, Sai, Rovo, and Aurora dashed around tentacles and splashed through goo trying to figure out how to hurt the thing. The whole scene felt like a bad flick, one where all the budgets went to special effects and nothing to the plot.

"Why is this thing even here?" Eponi said into the squad's channel between a warning call from Aurora to Rovo and a curse from Sai as his sword stuck again into the mud beast's side. "Out of this entire swamp, we happen to land right on top of it? What are the odds?"

She aimed the rifle as a tentacle swept up Gregor, pulling the big man towards the top of the beast's bulk. A yellow strip on her weapon's side shifted towards green as the rifle sucked spare electrons from the atmosphere, charging up its own batteries to launch death back out. The charging tech had started in weapons like this and then made its way to the racers she loved, leading to days-long contests where managing battery power took as much skill as navigating the course. The prize purses for those . . . she'd get back to them.

"You chose the landing spot!" Rovo bothered to reply.

"Kill it!" Aurora played her part, shut down irrelevant conversation. "Eponi, help Gregor."

Eponi squeezed off another yellow bolt towards the beast's top. It vanished into the mud with a sizzle, doing nothing to assist Gregor as the mud beast threw him into a nearby tree. Gregor hit the trunk, a rotting thing that looked more like a harbinger of horrors rather than a plant, and broke it, landing on the tree's gnarled roots below. Eponi grimaced—that looked like it hurt—and stood. Gregor didn't move, except for his right leg's slow slide towards the muck. Guess she could help him avoid drowning in the disgusting swamp.

With her boosters kicking, Eponi leapt off the drop shuttle's nose and flew over Sai's swinging blade, a sliding tentacle, and Rovo's scattershot rifle blasts. For a hot second, the roots seemed like they might be beyond Eponi's grasp, but, as ever, the helmet's calculations proved correct and Eponi landed right where the visor said she would. Racers had strict limits on their autopilots, their computer assists, so natural skill took precedence. Out here? The less DefenseCorp left in its soldier's hands, the better.

Really killed the thrill.

"You alive, big guy?" Eponi said, reaching Gregor and

dragging—with the help of energy augments in her suit—him away from the liquid. She sent the words through the touch-comm, a near field link that'd send the sound right to Gregor without muddling the squad's open channel. "Fight's still going. They could use your hammer out there."

A hammer that, Eponi noted, still occupied prime position in the mud thing's crown. Though it seemed like Sever had made some headway: much of the mud had been burned or cut away, revealing grassy-green scales and fur, as though the creature had blended species and chosen the ugliest parts. The fight's good news did nothing to spur Gregor; the man stayed still.

"Clear to wake him up?" Eponi tossed out to the channel.

"Clear!" came Aurora's reply.

"Sorry, buddy." Eponi pressed in on a tiny pair of notches beneath Gregor's helmet, against his neck.

Those notches ran a quick verification scan against Eponi's gloves, making sure she had friendly credentials. Her visor screen split into halves, the left green and the right red. Eponi winked with her left eye, and when the visor flashed all green for a microsecond, she let go of her teammate. Stepped back and watched as Gregor's suit hummed to a whining, glass-breaking sound. At the noise's apex, Gregor twitched, his hands and feet flaring out followed by a heavy sigh. His eyes opened, found Eponi's, and then shut again.

"I hate that," Gregor said on their near-field channel.

"How many times?"

"Lost count after a dozen."

Eponi stopped herself from noting DefenseCorp regs suggested all kinds of harmful effects linked to repeated shock-jock tech. Sever held a fuzzy relationship with

DefenseCorp, and that may as well extend to this too. Impossible missions demanded impossible compromises, or something like that.

The mud creature let out its first real noise of the fight, a gibbering, wet cough arising from its middle as Sai finally managed to get his sword through the creature's liquid sludge armor and cut into the good stuff. As death rattles went, Eponi had heard far better screams from pilots as their racers plummeted into endless crevasses or slipped into lava rivers.

Aurora and Rovo apparently agreed, taking advantage of the creature's distress to boost their way near Sai and concentrate their fire into the fresh wound. Like a poorly chosen microwave meal, the heat built up through the middle of the monster before it exploded, raining prodigious muck and worse all over the squad.

Except for Eponi, who'd taken Gregor's rise as an opportunity for cover and crouched behind the large man. Guts and glop splattered around everyone except her, and Eponi didn't give one single damn. She'd lived, made it one step closer to that pay day.

"LOOK AT YOU," Rovo said roughly five minutes later, as the squad turned to unloading essentials from the drop shuttle. Aurora tasked Eponi and Rovo with the foodstuffs, which they were throwing into expandable buoy-packs, so named for their negative pressure pockets designed to repel gravity enough to make heavy weights an easy carry. "All clean. The rest of us have some natural camouflage."

"Just doing my part," Eponi replied, shoveling micro-energy bars by the armful into one of the gray packs. "I'll draw all the fire."

"Fire from what?"

Eponi had already forgotten Rovo had the rookie disease—all threats were hypothetical, because Rovo hadn't experienced them yet. Not outside of a simulator, anyway.

"Did you miss the skiffs?"

"They weren't that dangerous, and we made it away from them." Rovo filled his pack to the brim and tugged on the taut string towards the top. The pull triggered the pack's closing mechanism, and the buoy-pack compressed around the more substantial meal packets Rovo had chosen, creating a rounded cube the rookie, with Eponi's help, slotted into a pair of back notches on his armor. "If that's all we're dealing with, minus the swamp monster, I think this ought to be simple."

"We don't get simple missions. Don't know what they told you when you signed on with Sever, but we're here to handle what DefenseCorp won't touch with its legitimate squads. That means high risk, high reward."

"Is that why you're here? The reward?"

Seeing someone's expression through their mask required x-ray vision, so Eponi couldn't quite tell whether Rovo had asked the question honestly or not. Then she realized she didn't care.

"I didn't choose to be here. That should tell you the reward isn't all that good," Eponi replied. "But Sever gets to stay away from the rest of DefenseCorp's crap, and they say we can ditch out whenever we want. No contracts, no clauses, no complaints. That's enough for me."

"Kind of hard to ditch out now."

Eponi finished her own pack, and as Rovo slapped it into place on her back, Aurora made the general evac call. Time to get away from the drop shuttle, march through the muck, and figure out where this VIP happened to get himself stuck.

"That's the real truth," Eponi said as she punched in the drop shuttle's self-destruct code. It'd take a couple hours to go off, long enough for Sever to get far enough away from any eyes attracted to the fire. "Once you're a part of Sever, there is no way out. Not alive, anyway."

TEN

Marsh March

SEEING a ship explode in the mustard green fog didn't make the kind of fireworks Rovo expected. He'd come out to DefenseCorp for the cash, and then joined Sever for the excitement when the cash proved stale, which happened fast when the only things he could spend it on were DefenseCorp merch.

Now, hours into his first mission with Sever, they'd just slaughtered some giant mud creature. He'd fired his rifle more times in the five-minute fight than he ever had before. Rovo could count plenty of choices he'd regretted in his life, but joining Sever, thus far, didn't number among them.

Rovo killed his manic grin when he and Eponi rejoined the squad, even though the helmet hid his mouth. His nerves, even after packing foodstuffs and dealing with the logistical boredom of plotting directions—Aurora did the plotting, Rovo did the waiting—still tingled. Adrenaline had his heart pumping. Rovo could've died back there. Smashed by one of those tentacles. How cool was that?

Going by the set faces and tired jokes from the rest, it

was, apparently, not cool. That's what you got with grizzled veterans. As the young kid, the new guy, the rookie, Rovo understood his place. He'd been here before—albeit in an office where the most dangerous weapon had been the coffee maker—and he'd probably be here again somehow. He endured Sever's hazing, their orders and everything else because this, already, had far eclipsed his life tailoring press releases and communiques for release across the galaxy. Now, instead of writing DefenseCorp's marketing, he would be the source for the stories.

"Rovo, you want front or back?" Aurora asked him as they clustered along the expensive dirt Gregor had used as a landing pad in the fight with the mud beast. Sever had cleaned off what mud they could, leaving green sludge patches on their armor like distorted badges of dubious honor.

"Front," Rovo replied. "If we meet something that talks, I'll be able to help more from there."

"We meet something that talks, you shoot first and figure out if it's a friend later," Gregor replied.

"You can't be serious?" Rovo said.

Sever's penchant for disregarding rules notwithstanding, blowing apart anything you met seemed like bad strategy.

"He's not," Aurora replied. "If any of you shoot before I give the clear, unless you're getting attacked, you'll be the one catching the laser from my rifle."

Aurora spoke with a hard steel edge Rovo found a little strange, seeing as she'd supposedly commanded this team for a while now. Why be so direct and rough with these guys? Weren't they all friends? But of all of them, Aurora did seem to have the best head for this. Rovo would rather have a hard-ass giving orders than a wild man like Gregor, who'd probably order a race to the objective, with whomever killed the most things along the way getting a bonus prize.

"You sure normal rules apply to this one?" Sai said. "We've already been shot at by the skiffs. We go in soft, we'll wind up dead."

"You don't know who those skiffs work for," Aurora replied. "For all we know, there's multiple factions at play here." Aurora did that leader thing, passing her stare around the whole group as she spoke, making sure everyone paid attention. "We don't have a ride off planet. We make enemies of everyone, we're stuck here. So keep those fingers off your triggers until I say so."

Rovo wanted to look over at Sai, but wearing a helmet designed to block lethal laser and projectile fire from any angle and, thus, blocking vision from all sides save straight ahead, he couldn't just flick his eyes that way. Visual systems in the armor would let him know of an imminent threat from out of sight, but they weren't any good for spying someone's reactions. Hard to be stealthy in armor like this, but then, maybe that helped with the honesty. Wearing this, you had to be blunt, had to be clear.

Gregor took point with Rovo when they trudged forth. The bigger man led, flipped his visor to scan for solids, which cut through the swamp water and allowed them to walk the shallowest path. Aurora pointed them towards the nearest energy source, figuring that held the best chance for clues as to what Dynas had beneath all this fog. While Gregor scanned for walkways, Rovo kept his visor watching heat, which the energy source gave off in big blooms; red, green blossoms, cut by the blue and black trunks of moss-covered trees. As to what structure would produce this sort of thing, a power plant came as the most obvious suggestion, but it could be a factory, some sort of swamp mine . . .

Or another creature, so huge and monstrous that Rovo would get a story to tell for the rest of his life. That'd be cool too.

Because right now, documents were the only thing Rovo could talk about. Scanning them endlessly for DefenseCorp in a spinning space station not far out of the Sol system. A structure that spent its time whirling between a whole collection of broadcast arrays meant to super-charge notices throughout known space. All sorts of orders for missions above and below board came and went, trans-lated and tossed off to respective governments and compa-nies. More than a few of them talking about objectives disguised as X or Y or Z. What Rovo had learned, what kept proving itself true: things never were what they seemed.

They were usually much worse.

Gregor moved through the swamp with all the subtlety of a drunken elephant. His footfall splashed wide arcs and he kept that hammer in his arms, swinging it back and forth like he was preparing to hit a ball, or feeling whether something invisible lurked in front of him. Rovo gave Gregor space, kept himself in the swampy mounds and root piles they used as land bridges making their way through the muck.

"What do you think?" Rovo said to Gregor. "Is this going to be a hard one?"

"We're having to walk," Gregor replied. "I already hate it."

"Why's that?"

Gregor took the invite. Went on and on about how most missions ought to be fiery and direct. A detonating landing into a storm where everything was hell for a few hours, then nothing left but rubble and victory. Trudging through anything was meant for infantry, for people more concerned with territory than singular objectives. The basic troops, in other words. Not the shining stars of DefenseCorp's special services. Not people like Gregor.

"DefenseCorp is turning into this, though," Rovo said once Gregor had finished his diatribe. "I saw so many places disband their own military and hire out. Defense-Corp isn't just guarding places or doing strikes anymore. It's fielding literal armies. Can't wait to see what happens when they're ordered to fight themselves."

"It's bad for business."

"Pretty good actually."

"No, my business," Gregor said. "You and I, we are tools. We should be used for what we are meant. Perhaps you are meant for slogging, perhaps you are meant to waste your time in a place like this. But me? I belong in the middle of things."

Sure. Because when Gregor went into the middle and the mud beast flung him around, that worked out so well. But Rovo held back. Rookies couldn't make statements like that, and Gregor had a really big hammer.

"I don't know," Rovo said. "I think we have to change if we want to keep our jobs."

"The job?" Gregor didn't turn. Didn't stop moving forward, but Rovo had the distinct impression that if Gregor had, Rovo would be staring up into a mean mug right now, a pair of disappointed eyes and a shaking head. "If this is a job to you, then you ought to be in front. Take all of the shots. Be the worker DefenseCorp wants. For me," Gregor patted the hammer head in his right hand, "for me this is life."

Cheesy sentiments. Rovo had written those too. Plenty of proclamations coming through the cables. Part of why he'd come out here, to get away from all that nonsense. He'd had it for a while with the swamp creature, but now

Rovo had an overactive filter trying to keep the air breathable. A creaky armor suit feeling heavier by the minute. Hunger he couldn't slake because he couldn't reach the pack on his back, and even if he could the swamp gave them nowhere to sit and eat. Rovo couldn't see more than a few meters in front of him without resorting to other visual spectrums. Exciting to be on a mission, sure, but hardly the stuff of dreams.

But if Gregor saw this as some sort of soul edifying enterprise, Rovo might be missing something. Time to see what.

"I'll take front if you want," Rovo said. "If you think I can."

Gregor held up his left hand. The whole column paused.

"Aurora," Gregor said. "The new kid wants to take point."

"Think he's ready?"

"No."

"New kid, you think you're ready?" Aurora asked.

"I volunteered, didn't I?" Rovo replied.

"You understand something kills you, we're not bringing your body back," Aurora said. "Too far away for an evac, even if we had one."

"I get it."

"Then let him have it Gregor." Aurora showed no reaction in her blaze red suit. "Just try to point out if you see something, let Rovo live a little longer."

And that's how Rovo found himself marching headlong through the fog, out of the swamp and into a whole new hell.

ELEVEN

Mine Games

AURORA WATCHED her rookie take his first steps leading the squad. Tentative, and then, when Rovo realized everyone waited behind him, faster. Aurora understood—she'd been a rookie once too. You had to take the first step sometime.

Now Aurora stayed towards the back with only Eponi behind her. Preserving some semblance of rank-and-file as they marched through the muck. The battle with the mud beast hadn't taken a lot out of her, though Aurora hadn't had to do much except fire her rifle and dodge a flailing tentacle or two. It'd been Gregor, Sai carrying the heavy weight.

But that's what commanders were supposed to do. Coordinate, plan and react. Keep the pieces where they ought to be.

And what a piece she'd become. Not at all according to anyone's plan, including her own.

After getting off-world in a hunt for adventure, Aurora had played her way through a variety of grunt jobs until her severe face and intimidating attitude—honed in a crowded house full of unruly siblings—earned the right second look from some regional manager who'd plopped her in charge of their local outlet plying small arms to the messy crowd who lived in a space station on the fringe.

Adventure aplenty there, especially whenever she had to refuse a sale to someone who seemed more likely to blow a hole in the station than use the weapon for any constructive purpose. Her cash account grew. Aurora sprinkled her dreams with a hint of daring. Until Defense-Corp shut them down.

Aurora's visor shifted its display as she ran her eyes along her team, tendrils of yellow mist floating between them. The squad's readings appeared in translucent blue numbers in front of her eyes, while Aurora kept her feet matching Sai's placement. Vital signs normal; Sever held it together after the beast. Even Sai, who kept thinking about his family, had himself feeling comfortable. Heartbeat, adrenaline. All good. Aurora couldn't be sure whether the signs were better or worse because of the fog—the soup made it impossible to see anything beyond in the normal spectrum, so you could either relax and accept the inevitable, or you could panic.

DefenseCorp, smaller back then, had started assessing and destroying its competitors. At that point, only the small fish. Shops like hers that supplied the means of defense to the everyday citizen, the local militias and hungry politicians who figured having a security force with teeth played better. Because let's face it, space scared people. Even the ones that ventured into it, like Aurora, did so because they had no other options. You didn't give up a comfortable spot in a nice town overlooking the ocean and risk a thousand terrible deaths because you had the itch to travel. You went to space, you did it because you had nothing to lose.

"Slower Rovo," Aurora said as the rookie made it several paces beyond Gregor to the point where he vanished from her own sight, his outline only visible in a light green on the HUD in front of her eyes. "You get too far away, we won't be able to help you."

Her free-fall after the shop's closure had been a quick one. Mostly because when you shut down a place filled with weapons, the employees aren't going to take it kindly. Aurora and a couple other employees, infuriated at the sudden destruction of their livelihoods, took some of the stock DefenseCorp hadn't purchased when they bought the store itself. Older models, but still plenty deadly.

Thus equipped, Aurora's makeshift squad marched through the station, causing plenty to turn the other way and walk a little faster. Another part of space life: every-one's got their own business and as long as you're not the target, you may as well ignore it. Someone else's problem, someone else's time.

Aurora hadn't been planning to actually assault DefenseCorp. Even in the nebulous world of space station justice, straight up blowing people to pieces tended to get you kicked out an airlock without a whole lot of debate, no matter what your argument. No matter how justified.

So when they arrived at the section bought and owned by DefenseCorp, its entrance painted in reds and blues, the logo in big block letters playing across the doors and a pair of musclebound guards standing in front, Aurora found herself paralyzed. The DefenseCorp guards, somewhat amused by the threat, decided to neutralize it by giving them what the whole crew really wanted: jobs.

If you could breathe and needed cash, DefenseCorp would take you.

"Heads-up," Gregor said. "We got something up front."

Rovo stopped and Gregor caught up with him,

standing at the start of what looked like a big fallen tree trunk.

"Gregor," Sai said, his voice catching the tight urgency the man always seemed to get whenever danger neared life and limb. "Do not move. There's a depth mine right there."

Aurora joined the group, stood amid a bundle of collapsed branches coated with whole platforms of moss and sludge. Mushrooms popped up too, their tops florescent blue. Perhaps something to make them visible in the thick air.

She couldn't see the depth mine, so Aurora flipped her visor to pick up energy signatures. Not quite heat, but rather the concentrated electron motion in a small space. A depth mine relied on signal disruption, and that signal appeared in a bright blue sliver that popped up above the swamp surface and then sank below to a little box crackling with energy. The sliver went straight through Rovo and Gregor's chosen route, sticking up through a large stone at the end of their fallen tree trunk. The only visible way forward, the only visible path right towards the bigger, brighter energy signature up ahead.

"What's a depth mine?" Rovo said over the comm.

"You brush that signal," Sai said, "you'll find out. But you won't like it when you do."

"Stay still Rovo till we decide on a course," Aurora said. Sai had told Rovo, effectively, the same thing, but sometimes commander had to reinforce the obvious, especially when a rookie was involved. "Check beyond. I'm getting smaller signatures."

Nobody would set a mine here with nothing to protect. Sure enough, now that Aurora looked for them, she saw dots aplenty. More mines, yes, but also signal trails leading to what looked like, in this energy-spectrum view, cool purple cubes seemingly floating in the air. Aurora guessed they were attached to trees, turrets waiting for a mine to go off to see targets in the murk. They could have been programmed to shoot anybody, but maybe those people in the skiffs came close by here. Couldn't have friendly fire. But the skiff riders would avoid the mines whereas any ground-based intruder wouldn't. A crude way to protect a place, but effective, especially if your primary threat came from swamp-dwelling creatures.

"Boss," Eponi said from behind. "We're about to walk into a minefield? What is this job?"

Aurora had been wondering that herself. They'd come under fire as soon as they came near Dynas, and Defense-Corp had given them a weak drop ship that'd barely made it to the surface. One faint signal to track and no other information to go on, no support. Had Aurora done something to get on DefenseCorp's bad side? Had Sever? DefenseCorp had been known to shift troublesome units to suicide missions as an easy way to get rid of problems, but Aurora didn't know why Sever would qualify for that sort of extreme elimination.

"I don't know," Aurora said. "But we're here now, and we're going to get off this rock together. Sai, can you take care of this one?"

"Maybe?" Sai said. "I need the rookie and Gregor to back up though. Real slow."

"I thought you just told me to stay still," Rovo replied.

"New orders," Aurora said. "Gregor you go first. One step at a time, and guide Rovo back with you."

"You're seeing those turrets right?" Eponi said. "I see six. If they activate, we're dead."

"They're tied to the mines," Aurora said. "We don't set one off, they won't shoot us."

The first DefenseCorp gig she'd had, probably just to

get her off the space station, had been to a frosted waste-land of a world where Aurora, along with a hapless squad, had been tasked with defending a mining installation from indigenous creatures.

Snarling ice-coated beasts with as many arms and claws as her nightmares could give them, they burrowed through the ice, traveling hordes attracted by the rumbling mining drills.

Aurora's squad had used depth mines just like this one. Planted them before every drill session, every night, and often woke up to explosions sending snowy geysers into the sky when the creatures attempted another attack. Aurora would bolt up, reach for her weapons, and by the time the habitat's door opened and the cold winds sapped the strength from her bones, there'd be dozens of the things slashing and snarling. She'd fire all night long, yellow lasers lighting up the dark till the far off triple stars brought daylight.

"You sure about that?" Eponi said. "If you're wrong, and I know I'm repeating myself but I feel like it's an important point to make, we're dead."

"I'm sure."

Fear could be a way to keep a squad together. The idea that if they split up, or gave in to panic, they would all die. That fear of death would keep the squad on target. Keep them ready for what the mission demanded. The problem with fear was that it spread like a poison. Aurora could see it starting, hear it in Eponi's voice, and in Rovo's shallow breathing that came through the transmission because he neglected to close his mic. Sloppy mistakes that led to worse outcomes which led to more fear. A vicious cycle ending with them all dead.

Aurora couldn't let that happen. Wouldn't. She kept her voice stable, issued the commands, guided Rovo and

Gregor back and told Sai to go forward. The demolitions expert would have his chance. Disarm the mine and they could move on.

If Sai failed?

Well, Aurora always had fear.

TWELVE

Depth Mine

OF ALL THE skills a father ought to teach his child, Sai figured demolitions and disarming had to number among the top five. At least in terms of usefulness, knowing how to take apart a computer, a vehicle, or, in this case, a depth mine, meant survival.

Life in space was a life wrapped in tech—knowing how to make it harmless or keep it from exploding were marketable skills. At least so far as DefenseCorp's pay indicated.

Not that Sai would have a chance to teach them to his kids anytime soon, or ever, thanks to physics and the vast distances between him and his family.

These thoughts buzzed around Sai's mind as he crept closer to the mine he'd been ordered to disable. Gregor and Rovo went back behind him, taking cover with Eponi and Aurora deeper in the swamp, giving Sai room to work. Also, of course, giving them distance so they wouldn't die if this mine happened to explode or trigger the turrets to melt Sai in the middle of this desolate mire.

Of all the planets to get stuck on, Dynas had the dubious privilege of being the worst Sai had ever seen.

Deserts, verdant forests, even ocean worlds where society functioned on vast floating cities, Sai had seen'em and loved'em all. Taken pictures with his visor and tossed them in the digital maelstrom beaming back and forth across the galaxy to his family. After a few years or more, his kids might get a glimpse of what their father was up to. Thankfully, they'd see it before they died, as life expectancy pushed people into the multi-century span, unless you were a moron like Sai and jumped into a combat career. Which, maybe, his kids already had . . .

The mine. That's where Sai needed to focus. Up close, Sai could see the thing had been embedded into the base of a moss-coated rock. The fat tree Sai stood on led right up to the stone, though he couldn't see anything continuing on the other side. So the thinking went somebody walking on their way tripped the mine and fell into the swamp as all the turrets came alive and roasted their hapless body? Not the most sophisticated trap, but it might work.

Rovo had nearly tripped it, right?

"Are you going to move or what?" Eponi asked. "I don't know about you, Sai, but I don't like this planet. There are other places I'd rather be."

"I take my time because if I don't we all die," Sai countered. "If you want to try it go right ahead."

"I wouldn't want to show you up."

Sure. That made sense.

Sai crept closer, dipping up to his waist in the muck, crawling towards the mine. As he neared the end, the log came to a point, forcing Sai to his hands and knees, gripping the mossy log with a hug and squirming closer.

Up close, the mine, thanks to some silvery lumps the moss hadn't yet coated, revealed some secrets. Namely, the mine wouldn't just trigger the turrets. It had a full base, packed into the back of the stone where some enterprising engineer had carved away the rock to nestle in a surprise package. Looked, too, like this particular mine, and possibly the whole defense system, was pretty new, and good thing for Sai: too much later and all the mine's visible pieces would be covered by the glistening green moss growing over every available spot.

To disarm the mine, though, Sai needed to get behind it, to the explosives and where the mine's little power pack would be stored. Without that pack, the mine couldn't send any info to the turrets, and they'd be safe. The mine might still explode, but if Sai took care of the power and someone still stepped on this thing, then it was their own fault. Sai flipped his visor to a polarized view that cut through the swamp water and gave him a good idea of the depth, see whether he could step around the mine.

"Almost twenty meters deep over here," Sai said. "Be careful where you step."

"I thought you liked to swim?" Gregor said, the suit sending Gregor's voice right to Sai's ear, sounding like Gregor had moved right next to him and asked the question.

"I do, just not wearing dozens of kilograms of armor. Not all of us are built like trucks."

"Whose problem is that?"

Sai missed the early days, when Gregor kept his mouth shut and played the strongman role to perfection. Now he kept trying to be clever, and he'd developed enough cockiness to go along with the big hammer of his. Annoying. But then, every squad had its issues, and Sever's weren't as bad as most. At least Sever was effective. At least Sai knew Gregor wouldn't run away from a fight.

Speaking of fights, he had to get past this mine.

Maybe, if Sai held on to the end of the log, he could get down in the swamp and move around the mine and find something to hang onto over there. The rock and its mine stood at just over half a meter in length. Big enough to grab, but not small enough to pick up and move. Sai reached forward, put his hands on the stone and shifted his legs, ready to drop in and pull himself around. As Sai moved his right leg forward, he leaned on his hands, pushing them into the moss to get a hard grip on the stone.

The mine beeped. A warning. Of course they'd put pressure sensors all around the stone. Sai's hands probably didn't have the weight to set it off right away—you wouldn't want mines exploding for small animals—so the beep ought to scare them off.

"Don't worry," Sai said, removing his hands and scooting back on the log. "It's going to be a little tricky."

"Why should we worry?" Rovo said. "We're way back here."

Demolitions. The best skill. The best role.

"Can you stop talking and get moving?" Aurora said. "I don't want those skiffs to catch us waiting."

Fine. So Sai couldn't use the rock as ballast. Thankfully, these armors came with plenty of gear. Sai took a link line, cinched to a clamp on his waist, and stabbed it the end into the tree trunk where it snagged a solid hold. He tested it with a couple of yanks, figured that if he jumped off and the whole tree broke away, well, at least Sai tried. Having done that, Sai glanced up at the yellow mist above and wished he had a better sky to say goodbye to.

Sever didn't get to choose their moments of bravery or where they occurred, they just had to go regardless.

Sai slid off the log, and sank. He reached out for anything to hold onto, but he kept going down. A deep part of the swamp. Through his visor, Sai saw little green spots as plants drifted by on the slow current. A blue-white counter appeared across the top of his vision, showing his oxygen level. The suit assumed Sai wanted to go underwater, and took the necessary precautions, none of which would stop Sai from drowning at the bottom of Dynas's damned marsh, though they'd keep him alive long enough to regret it.

The link line came to his rescue when it reached its max. Like coming to land on a thick, fluffy bed, Sai bobbed under the grimy sea.

"Need help?" Aurora asked.

"Doing fine."

"Doesn't look like it," Eponi added.

"Could say the same about you." Sai wasn't sure if that qualified as a good comeback, but in his present state, he didn't care.

The switch to retract the link line sat inside the clamp, so Sai reached around and flipped it, starting a slow pull to the surface. As he rose, Sai swam with his bulky armored covered arms. He didn't move too far, didn't move too fast, but he made it beneath the mine's rock and to the other side, managing to reach back and flip the switch, stopping the link line's retraction as he breached the surface, as he found a new sandbar a half-meter or so beneath the water to stand on. Sai let out some slack to keep his own grapple from sucking him back into the depths, then blinked at what he saw.

Through the haze, he could make the outline of a large building, its top vanishing into the mist. The swamp drained out considerably too, turning from water to mud and mossy rock in short order beyond the mine. Close enough, almost, to jump from the rock to the shallows. A temptation that would have an eager visitor triggering his doom without a second thought.

"We're almost to the building," Sai said. "I'm on the other side of the mine, so I'm going to disarm it now."

"Nice work." Aurora again. "Let's arm up. Once we get a path to the building, we're going to take it."

Sai turned back to the mine. He blinked and swapped his visor over to an X-ray view, where he could see the light blue lines indicating the borders of the mine's explosive housing. Covered in the moss, but there. Now the trick would be getting his hands in position to open it without putting too much weight on the top of the rock. If he put both hands against the moss, Sai wouldn't have a free one to open the housing and remove the power pack. If he didn't put both on the rock to stabilize himself, then Sai would slip back beneath the water.

He needed a third option. And he had one. Sai took a slow jump off of the sandbar, drifting towards the mossy rock. He had one chance or Sai would sink back down, but he couldn't go too fast or he'd trigger the mine.

Sai angled his head and mashed his visor against the rock's back. His helmet stuck in the moss, green goo coating his vision. But his helmet held, the moss giving enough purchase so that, along with his right hand, Sai managed an ugly support to keep him afloat. An awkward hug, but a workable one.

The mine stayed quiet. He lived.

Now to the real work. Sai snapped his left wrist and engaged the multitool. The little device, every Sever member had one, held laser cutters, screwdrivers, and other simple gadgets. First, Sai swapped to a microlaser. He blazed a path through the moss using his left hand, almost like pointing a beam from his finger. Bright white and hot, the moss recoiled, burned black at the edges, a charred smell in the air. Beneath the growth, the mine's back hatch, no larger than Sai's own palm, sat waiting to be opened.

"Almost have it," Sai said. "But I need someone ready in case there's a dead switch on this."

"Dead switch?" Rovo asked.

"Sometimes you can rig stuff like this to go off if there's no power anymore," Sai said. "It's dangerous, because it means you can't touch the mine once it's placed, but I don't know who we're dealing with."

"I will get you," Gregor said, and while Sai couldn't see the man come closer from his current rock-mash point of view, he felt a little better.

Not that Sai expected to survive if the mine exploded, but maybe, just maybe.

Sai flipped the multitool to the wedge drive, a nano piece made to open tight flaps like this. With its edge going down to the molecular level, Sai pressed the wedge drive against the mine's plate and flexed left. Sai couldn't see the thing spring open but he could feel the pop. One more step accomplished.

Now Sai had to see inside, and that meant getting his helmet off the edge of the rock. Slow, easy, Sai pulled back from the clutching moss to get his head free. His left hand reached into the edge of the mine, in the open space created by the panel, and with his right hand's grip on the stone, Sai managed to get a good view inside. A simple long-life battery, and the explosive packs tied, with a zillion little wires leading out to those pressure sensors. Sai had to cut those first, then deal with the power pack.

He lifted his left hand, meaning to snap back to the microlaser. Bad call. The sudden weight slid his right hand off the moss, and when Sai tried to catch himself, he reached with his left, grabbed the explosive packs, and tore them out of the mine as he fell into the water. And that, more than anything, saved him. Submerged, Sai stared at the sodden mass of ripped explosives as their powders leaked, useless, into the muck. How about that? Not exactly the plan, but a good disarming had a lot of luck to it.

Sai resurfaced, his mouth already opening to deliver his affirmation of a good deed done, when deadly energy's sonic chorus stopped him flat. Like the worst horde of mosquitoes ever heard, the turrets all around them powered up. Why? Because Gregor stood there, his hammer driven right where the mine had been.

"I said I'd save you," Gregor said, pulling his hammer from the wreck.

"We're all gonna die," Sai replied.

THIRTEEN

Making An Entrance

SMASH ONE PROBLEM and you create a dozen more. Nobody ever said that, but Gregor thought it as his hammer completed its swing through the mine's metal-and-rock bulk, scattering components everywhere. As smashes went, this one wasn't particularly satisfying; the mine was too small. It lacked a living target's squishy bits. But one thing you learned quick when you had a hammer, was that you didn't get upset about the opportunity to smash, no matter what you were destroying.

The turrets, though, didn't seem inclined to let Gregor enjoy the moment.

"Get Sai out of there and let's go," Aurora's voice came hard over the team channel. "The building's just ahead, we can't face all of these."

Gregor would've liked to try, but he didn't give the orders. And, deep down, Gregor knew he shouldn't. So he reached out with his hammer, dove it into the muck and when he felt Sai wrap his hands around it, Gregor pulled up as the first bolt struck the log at his feet.

As the first bolt blew apart the rotting wood Gregor stood upon.

Sai's link line went flying as Gregor slid into the water, before pulling himself up one-handed—his right would only drop the hammer if he died—onto the rock remnants that had held the mine. Around them, the swamp liquefied as hot laser rained down. As if Dynas itself had armed and decided Sever would be its first and only target.

"We need cover!" Rovo hunkered down behind a tree, waving his rifle around, searching for a target in the misty morass.

"No, you need to move," Aurora replied and Gregor barely had a chance to get himself on the rock before the three of them blew past him, the boot boosters on their armor suits carrying them over Sai and Gregor, sending them in long leaps towards mossy mounds meters away. The three landed with all the grace you'd expect from ungainly armored soldiers leaping through gas and laser fountains. Rovo slipped off stones to crash face first in the muck, getting Aurora tangled as she fell towards the same shallows, before crashing through it and disappearing beneath the water. Eponi landed on her feet, mud and sludge scattering everywhere. Sai wasn't far behind, scrambling into the sand and pulling himself along through the reedy groves.

Gregor had a better plan.

With his hammer in his right hand, Gregor crouched on the rock and boost-jumped up, swinging his hammer overhead and catching a thick branch on the hammer's head. The weapon hooked and Gregor flung himself forward, like some mythical hero. Coupled with his boosters, Gregor flew far enough to pass over his squad mates and make the lucky first landing on real ground leading up to the structure.

The building, this close, revealed itself as far more than a small outpost. Like the mine, it's gray-black walls were overgrown with moss and bigger things—Gregor could swear whole trees erupted from its nooks and crannies—as though someone had never cleaned the building since its first construction. Lights crackled from within, giving their white glow to the mist.

Not empty, then.

Off to the left, in a cleared section, sat a floating landing pad with enough room for several skiffs. From the pad went a wide metal ramp with support struts submerged deep into the marsh, leading to what seemed like the structure's main door and the only part of the building that looked like it'd been used recently. Gleaming from the humid air, the door looked stable, built for deliveries, not assaults. What Sever had here was not a power station, but a full on base, one whose roof reached several stories high and that, by the look of it, continued further down beneath the surface.

If Dynas had been a boring, backwater world before, well, it still was, but at least the mission was getting more fun.

Stinging pain splashed away his concentration; Gregor took a hit in the leg. His armor deflected most of it, but the lasers were hot enough to send their heat part way through. The suit reported a possible second-degree burn on his skin. Which meant Gregor had to move. The others splashed up behind him as Gregor took his first lumbering lunge towards the door. They ought to have been dead by now from the turret fire, but as they moved, the lasers continued to strike around them at odd angles. Maybe the mist caused them to miss, or maybe they were too old and malfunctioning. Either way, Gregor wasn't going to complain. Surviving in this game took as much luck as it did skill, and today, after so much bad luck, they deserved a bit of the good.

"I'll break the door," Gregor said, bringing the hammer back into its two-handed grip as he crashed towards the entrance.

Even with the pain from his leg, Gregor loved this moment. Adrenaline surged. A clear target with the smell of ozone and battle thick in the air. The only thing that could make it better would be a few more things to crush.

As if hearing Gregor's wish, the mist around them moved, blown by artificial means. Two skiffs swooped down, loaded with soldiers. From the drop shuttle, and through the cannon's lens, Gregor hadn't been able to get a great look at what their enemies were wearing, but from here, up close as the targets jumped off their skiffs and landed in the shallows, he could see a webbed synthetic mesh coating them. A bodysuit, then. Gear aimed for functionality over Sever's hard-core protection, but to each their own. Maybe they had some special ventilation for the swamp air.

Several morons, drawing rifles from shoulder slings, dashed to cut Gregor off from the door. A bold move. A foolish move.

Gregor, now less than five meters away, activated the boosters and jumped. The skiff guards must not have expected a large man in gray-blue armor to spring three meters into the air, because their first shots woefully underestimated his height and blitzed beneath Gregor into nothing. Their defense did as little: the soldiers raised their weapons, tried to track where Gregor would fall and realized he was about to fall on them. He landed on the first while swinging his hammer in a wide arc from left to right, catching the other two and bashing them to the ground.

Squishy, sodden sand sucked in the bodies.

Gregor flipped a glance towards the skiffs, but Sever had started carrying their own weight, and the lasers from their rifles had the skiff soldiers crouching, fumbling, for defense. Gregor had a clear shot at the door and, with one good kick to knock out the man he'd landed on, a wheezing guard, Gregor completed the last few meters to his target. He raised the hammer and smashed it against the large door. The weapon banged off with a loud ring that echoed over the combat and sent a shivering jolt down through the handle, along with Gregor's arms, with enough verve to make his whole body vibrate.

Gregor would've lost the grip on the hammer if not for his own armor's efforts to keep his hands glued to the powerful weapon. A modification he'd made after a similar mission on X-29, a world made and run by out-dated robots, where the shivering had grown so strong after consecutive whacks to break into a bot factory's manufacturing gate that Gregor had broken both his wrists.

Now he held on, now he raced to a second strike and as he did so twisted the handle's base. The kinetic energy from the last few swings—the mine rock coming first—had the hammer ready to go, and this time, when it connected, the force of a dozen metric tons crashed into the door and blew it back off its supports. The great gate crashed inward, landing in the entry space with a loud, immensely satisfying thud.

Gregor hefted the hammer back, looked at his results, and announced, "Sever, we have our entrance."

FOURTEEN

Acrobatics

NOTHING LIKE A THREE-ON-DOZEN CHARGE. Eponi let Aurora take the lead as they splashed through the sandy mud towards the skiffs and the soldiers pouring off of them. Pressed to describe their uniforms, Eponi would say they looked like the aquatic outfits from Vitara, a watery planet where everyone sported wetsuits to keep the moisture from turning the populace into prunes. Dynas, seemingly one giant swamp, may as well be the more disgusting version.

None of that, though, stopped Eponi from shooting away with her pistol. Her yellow blasts mingled with the white bolts from the turrets—which were, in her estimation, the most inaccurate turrets she'd ever seen—and the enemy's orange fire to create a beautiful light show accompanied by the screams of the wounded and possibly dying. Not that Sever numbered in that batch. Eponi felt her armor take hits here and there, the laser burn searing through to her legs and arms, but unless she took repeated shots to the same spot, she ought to live.

DefenseCorp, and Sever, prepped for this. Their

missions guaranteed firefights. Sever's gear all-but guaranteed they'd make it out the other side.

And so when Rovo sprinted past her, a close-range laser pistol in each hand spraying wildly towards the skiffs, as though attempting to cut down his enemies by the sheer number of bolts fired rather than where those bolts happened to strike, Eponi let him go. Adjusted her angle so Rovo's bulky armor and the provisions pack he carried from the drop shuttle served as makeshift cover while his running-and-gunning pulled guards from the rightmost skiff towards the building to cut him off.

Rookies had to learn from their mistakes, and rushing ahead of the team most definitely qualified.

Eponi knew from her racing days that she'd get better laps around an unfamiliar track by spending the first go-round following the most familiar pilot. They'd know where to slow down, where to speed up, shortcuts and so on. Then, the next time around, she'd boost past them and take the lead. An easy win. At least, that's how it went in her head. How it would go when she earned the scratch to get back to the circuit.

While Rovo wasn't the most experienced, he could still show Eponi what not to do.

"Take the left!" Aurora said to her, the leader sending the communication direct through the linked channels and overriding Eponi's plan. "Rovo and I will keep their attention. You get flanking duty."

Necessary, because it looked like the soldiers were assembling an energy wall along the ramp up to the building's main entrance where . . . Gregor charged with a hammer. The guards seemed to be ignoring the man, and Eponi spied three crushed corpses making a compelling argument why. Sai, abandoning Captain Hammer, joined up with the three of them, adding his own rifle to their chorus that, for the moment, kept the enemy behind their growing cover.

The energy wall caught laser bolts and sucked away their power, charging the field's batteries with every shot. To flank a defensive stand like this, Eponi had to get left and do it without being seen. Her next step splashed up the muck and gave her an idea. Sometimes the best move meant faking the worst.

"Going," Eponi said. "Cover me."

She dove forward, flailing her hands as she fell, looking like she'd either been shot or lost all coordination. In the laser swarm, anyone would bet the former. Eponi crashed beneath the murky slime and tried to get as low as possible, her visor's oxygen meter serving as the clue that she'd submerged to a sufficient degree. Then she pressed her arms and legs against the sandy bottom, propelling herself at a slow, but constant speed that ought to make little impression on the surface. Keep the soldiers in the dark as long as possible.

"Hurry," Aurora's words came through with a little static from the liquid interference. "We're exposed, but Gregor has the door open. Once you get us a chance, we'll break for the building."

Eponi wanted to say it hadn't been her call to make the reckless charge across the soggy marsh, but she kept her mouth shut. Aurora had always been the striker type, figuring a strong offensive beat out a cowardly defense in every situation. A tactic that often fit Sever's outnumbered, outgunned and pursued mission structure pretty well; if they stopped moving, Sever should wind up dead. But here? On this foggy world where anyone would have trouble putting together a coherent response? Sever could have sat behind trees, picked off the guards and turrets from cover, and had a nice go of it.

Instead, Eponi pulled herself up on the landing pad, near the second, farther, skiff. She had to use the boot boosters to get her up and over—not that Eponi didn't have plenty of good, old-fashioned muscle, but these suits were damned heavy—and those same boosters gave her an unexpected, squealing scoot along the rubbery, floating pad until she banged her helmet into the bottom of the skiff. Rattled her skull good, but how many times had she shaken herself to a near stupor pulling some move on the circuit?

The silence cut Eponi, though. If nobody from Sever saw her slide-and-bump, if none of them called her on it, then the squad must really be in trouble. She looked up and over the nose of the skiff, caught the lay of things. The guards had completed their energy field line, and used it now to stand up and send sizzling bolts towards Rovo, Aurora, and Sai, who'd hunkered down behind a steadily melting rock in the middle of the approach.

Sever's counterfire lacked as the enemy's suppression proved near total. The rock, too, failed to provide cover from several turrets that seemed to be getting ever closer with their white-hot bolts. A look towards the building showed Gregor had definitely bashed in the door, but a few guards had him pinned inside, with Gregor blindly squeezing out shots without risking his bulk.

Eponi preferred saving the squad through impeccable piloting, but given the situation, she'd have to get messy. She threw her pistol back in its holster, and reached over her back to the locked in assault weapon clinging to her armor. At her touch, the assault rifle popped free and Eponi pulled it over, catching the barrel grip in her left hand. Thank goodness for energy weapons—Eponi had played with projectile arms before, and they, with their bulky clips and heavier metals, made moves like this so much harder. The weapon didn't exactly feel feather-light, but Eponi had no trouble aiming it down the guards line and holding the trigger. Gas ionized, heated, and launched itself in bright bolts that crashed into the crouching, calm guards.

Their blue-black suits burst open with orange fire as Eponi struck home, laying low five soldiers in the first few seconds. The others reacted quick, throwing themselves off the ramp into the swamp water and abandoning their fortification. One managed to spit a shot her way, the bolt striking the skiff's nose and leaving a charred mark on the otherwise ugly-as-all-hell green and brown coating.

"There's your opening," Eponi said, continuing to stitch fire around the ramp's edges to discourage any bravery.

"Making the break. Keep cover, then swap once we make the building." Aurora led the charge herself, again, the trio climbing and running past the rock towards the opening.

Figured Eponi would go last. With the guards subdued, Eponi swiveled around and sniped some of the pathetic turrets, blowing the cubes out of the trees and sending their flaming wrecks into the water. DefenseCorp made the assault rifles for crowd clearing, not accuracy, but when the target didn't move, even a weapon like this could get the job done.

"Ready, Eponi," Aurora said.

The signal given, Eponi slipped the assault rifle back into its slot in her armor and broke around the nose of the skiff. The guards didn't wait for a better moment, either, but shouted that opportunity had arrived and started their own scrambles onto the landing pad. Aurora and Rovo gave Eponi some cover fire, pulling their own rifles out and laying down enough blue bolts that Eponi felt like she ran through an aquatic explosion. The soldiers sent haphazard, missing lasers after her, and after several long seconds and longer strides, Eponi stepped over the broken door and into the base's loading dock.

Supply crates littered the broad area, with the immediate space beyond the door kept clear for new transports to unload, turn, and exit. Beyond that range, the ribbed crates, color-coded to clue folks into their contents, sat in stacks, waiting for someone to pick them up on a return journey to wherever on Dynas served as this base's support. The sheer size of the loading bay, bigger than some of the racer hangars Eponi had used, spoke to how big this building must be. This many supplies meant a lot of staff, meant a lot of work to keep this place running.

And running was what Sever ought to be doing, but once she made it past Aurora and Rovo, there didn't seem to be anywhere else to go. Gregor and Sai were at the one door leading further in, one quite a bit smaller than the main entrance, and apparently reinforced enough that Gregor's hammer couldn't break it. At least, that's what Eponi gathered when she saw Gregor pound the hammer into the floor and curse.

"You can't cut through with that thing?" Gregor asked Sai, who didn't draw his blade in response.

"It can cut metal fine," Sai said, "but it's not getting through something that thick."

To the right of the door, jutting out from the wall, sat what appeared to be a control room with narrow windows. Out of them, looking smug, stared a guard dressed in what seemed like a more normal emerald green uniform. He watched Gregor and Sai playing with the door, and Eponi watched him. The only reason the guard could look that unconcerned with a bunch of heavily armed and armored enemies in his base would be because he expected invulnerability. If Sever couldn't break further in, they would run out of energy eventually. Reinforcing skiffs full of fresh guards could mop them up.

"We need a new plan," Gregor said. "We are trapped."

"Then find a way out," Aurora replied. "Rovo and I can't keep them pinned forever."

Eponi kept looking, but she didn't see any open vents. No other doors or ways to punch open. Gregor picked up the hammer and swung it at a random point in the wall, causing a good dent, but nothing more.

"You have any big bombs?" Eponi asked Sai. "Blow us a hole?"

"If Gregor's hammer can't break through, I'd need a pretty big explosive," Sai replied. "We couldn't stay in here, and I'm not going back out there."

As if to put truth to Sai's words, bolts began zapping through past Aurora and Rovo, who called out that a third skiff had just landed outside. The situation wasn't getting better, which meant they had to go with unusual tactics.

"Gregor," Eponi said, pointing to the windows and the guard's face. "Break that."

Gregor, in his big gray blue armor, stared at her for a second before shrugging. He took two long steps before leaning in to a wide, arcing blast into the window and the backpedaling guard behind it. The hammer destroyed the glass, scattering shards everywhere.

"Way too small," Sai said.

"For you, maybe," Eponi replied. Circuit racers had to be tiny—less weight and size made for smaller, sharper craft—and Eponi figured she had a chance at fitting through the slit. Only thing, she couldn't keep her armor on to do it. "Cover me."

Eponi clomped near the window while both Gregor and Sai drew their spitters and kept the guard inside cowering. With her back to the solid wall, watching Aurora and Rovo exchange increasingly desperate fire with the guards outside, Eponi triggered her armor's exit commands. She pressed in a pair of slight buttons on her waist, and with a series of clicks, her armor unlatched itself, unfolding away from her like the peel on a particularly ripe fruit. Designed to travel on tight ships, her yellow suit followed its own algorithm to pack and press itself tight, compressing into a box not all that much larger than the backpack full of provisions she'd taken from the drop ship and set down next to her. A scant few seconds later, Eponi stood with only her slim skinsuit, handing her laser pistol to Gregor.

"Ready?" Sai said, actually projecting his voice through his suit's speakers, as Eponi no longer had any way of accessing the squad's channel without her helmet.

"Ready." Eponi stepped back from the window, sized up the opening. It would be tight, but she could make it. "Now!"

She sprinted, jumped, and thanked her skinsuit as it protected her hands from the remaining glass shards lining the window's edges like jagged teeth. Eponi pulled herself up, slid through, and caught her laser pistol as the big man tossed it to her while she completed the fall. The guard inside had time to look at her and start to say something before she fried him.

"Nice toss," Eponi said to Gregor, who raised the hammer in reply.

The control room kept things simple. A series of clear buttons, no real console. Stunningly low-tech, but then, it seemed this base was out in the middle of nowhere. More complicated systems meant more points of failure, and if you couldn't have reliable maintenance . . . Eponi had always laughed at the circuit racers who thought their super fancy ships gave them an advantage. They'd blow their nav system to a micro-asteroid or miss-time their million jets and send their max-price toy into oblivion, and often themselves along with it.

"I have our escape," Eponi said, tapping away at the panel and smiling as the resultant clanks and thunks sent the loading dock's sole interior exit open.

"I've got your armor," Sai said, holding it as he and Gregor thudded towards the opening. "Come get it, please."

"On my way," Eponi glanced back to the guard. Wondered if he had anything she should take—he wore a badge, and another door, leaving the control room, looked like it had one of those security scanners.

"Let's go, Eponi!" Aurora shouted. "We're pulling back!"

Wouldn't do them any good to get trapped again. Eponi reached down, pulled the guard's badge off, and turned back to the window when laserfire cascaded through and Eponi flung herself to the ground as hot energy stitched a glowing line on the walls around her.

"I need an opening!" Eponi called.

No reply, but the fire coming her way died out, so Eponi risked a glance. Sever had vanished from the loading bay, though at least two of her squad mates kept up some fire from their new door. Guards in those wetsuits streamed through the main entrance, all but ensuring Eponi a swift death if she made an unprotected leap through the window. Change of plans, then. A new route. She reached over, reversed the buttons she'd pressed earlier and slammed Sever's new door shut. Then Eponi blasted the controls, slagging the buttons.

Return fire came her way, so Eponi crouched, shimmied over to the door and stuck the badge to the scanner, praying it would open. With a beep, it did, showing a small hallway on the other side. Alone, unarmored, and with only her trusty laser pistol for protection, Eponi went through.

A racer had to roll with the unexpected.

FIFTEEN

Rookie Move

JUST LIKE THAT, Sever had gone down to four. Eponi had disappeared through that window while Rovo dropped his smoke grenade and she hadn't come back out. In all the movies, the hero always gets away after making the big play, but Rovo had to stop telling himself this wasn't like that. They were dealing with real consequences here, not just a game. So when Gregor handed Rovo Eponi's armor, which had compressed itself to a neat, rectangular package, Rovo actually had to carry it.

"She'll need it," Gregor said.

"It'll lock into your backpack," Sai said, coming up behind Rovo while Aurora covered the small, now-closed door leading back to the loading bay.

Gregor adopted the lead role, a position his hammer earned for him, a position nobody cared to fight him for. The corridor they'd gone into had substantial width over a normal hallway, big enough for supply carts to trundle down, but compared to the open swamp, It felt awful similar to the space stations Rovo lived on for so long. Not a feeling he cared to return to, but he guessed the familiarity helped quell the panic that'd been growing ever since those turrets started firing at him.

His right shoulder hurt, and Rovo knew his left knee would need some attention. He didn't know whether it'd been the guards or the turrets that had pegged him as Rovo had made the final run towards the base, but those flashes had come with as much surprise as they had pain. Simulations never nailed that part—they could get the battles perfect, the visuals amazing, but the actual feeling of taking a shot? DefenseCorp had a long way to go before they'd knock their trainee's fear away. Only Aurora's steel presence, and the thought of Gregor's hammer dealing a deserter their fatal blow, kept Rovo in line now.

Rovo's subtle panic didn't just reside in his mind. His hands twitched, sweat poured out of everywhere even though his suit kept his temperature ideal. Rovo's stomach churned, and he kept clenching his hands on his rifle trigger, as though the weapon could somehow save him from where he'd wound up. The swamp creature had been exciting, a strange thrill to begin the adventure, but these guards? They weren't bad dreams, they were actually trying to kill him.

If Rovo couldn't pull himself together soon, they'd probably succeed.

Sever passed by the entrance to what looked like a mess hall, conveniently close to where someone would unload food, before continuing to a circular intersection. Hallways split to the left and right, while dead ahead a large sliding door had its chromed face coated with a deep green 1. On that door's sides, shock white floor numbers painted chromed panels, embedded into buttons. Looked like a lift that could go up or down a single story.

"Any guesses?" Sai asked. "You ever get any blueprints in that communications job, Rovo?"

"Not of places like this," Rovo replied. "Secret bases on hidden planets tend not to go through official channels."

"We split up." Aurora cut in, walked into the center of the circle and inspected the door. "I'm not assuming Eponi's dead till we find her body, but we also need to find a way out of this base that doesn't involve going back to those skiffs."

"Wait, you want us to split up?" Rovo said. "With all those guys back there?" Sever looked at Rovo, their helmets hiding expressions that the rookie could guess weren't very complimentary. "Look, I know I'm new, but you can't seriously be thinking that wandering around this place in small groups is the right plan?"

Aurora turned back around, faced Rovo directly. "Rovo, I welcome your input, but when I give an order, I expect it to be followed without disagreement. You're armored, you have heavier weapons than they do. Small corridors favor us, because we can't get surrounded." She half-turned back to the lift. "We're on a planet we don't know, fighting a force we don't understand. Split up, find Eponi and a way out. Learn what you can about this place too, it might help us find the VIP."

Rovo had forgotten about the target. What with everything else, covering the planet to rescue whomever sent that first signal seemed like the height of lunacy. Already his rifle ran low on its power pack, and while Sever had spare energy, fighting like this would leave them burnt out and empty before long. Whatever goal they'd had at the start, Sever couldn't achieve it now, not without some major changes.

"I'll take the rookie and we'll find Eponi," Sai said. "You get us an exit."

Sai? Why'd the demo dude want to roll with Rovo?

Again, the damn helmets hid expressions, so Rovo had to assume Sai had lost some sort of bet. Neither Aurora nor Gregor argued with the call, and the latter slapped the lower floor on the lift. Why down instead of up? Rovo didn't know, but he'd already been chewed out by Aurora once in this conversation and didn't care to get hit again.

"Good," Aurora said. "We'll tell you when we've found something. You do the same."

Rovo waited approximately three minutes after they'd left the intersection, with Aurora and Gregor vanishing inside the lift, to ask Sai why he'd chosen to go with the rookie. They were moving slow down the right hallway, which seemed like it might reconnect with Eponi's route. Doors lined the space, closed and sporting badge scanners. Sai could have blown them open, or maybe sliced them with his sword, but Eponi probably wasn't hiding in some random room. Sai had also taken the lead, a cautious walk with his rifle out and aiming forward. Rovo knew enough to swing back every now and then as they passed beneath the ceiling's small, white lights to check their sixes.

"Why? Because I was a rookie once too," Sai said. "Figure I'd pass along the favor another guy did for me. I know it's scary out here, your first mission like this."

Sentiment? Warmth from a Sever?

"It's . . . hard," Rovo admitted.

"Best advice I can give you? Don't get caught up in the emotion. Save that for later," Sai replied. "Right now it's all about survival, and if you want to do that, you have to keep calm."

"Guess I shouldn't be surprised to hear that from a bomb guy."

"From anyone that's survived more than a couple missions. Usually the solution to a problem, even a firefight, isn't to keep shooting. You have to know where to aim, find the weakness."

"Now you're just spouting cliches."

"They're cliches for a reason. They'll keep you alive."

The hallway took a sharp bend to the left, and they hit another door, this one painted over with radiation's telltale yellow sign. A badge scanner on this door, too. Sai stood in front of the entrance as Rovo caught up to him. He tried to figure out what Sai looked at, but couldn't guess.

"Do you know what's strange?" Sai said, still staring at the barrier. "There's no alarm going off in here. The lights are all their normal hue. No evacuation, no calls to arms. A base like this, you'd think there'd be a whole crew in here fighting us."

"There was the guy that Eponi took out."

"One? No, way too few." Sai reached out, pushed Rovo back a step. "Give me some room. I'm going to cut this open."

"Of all the doors, you're choosing the one with the radiation sign?"

"Look at it. The door's too thin to block anything really dangerous. Whatever's behind this might be able to cause a problem, but it's not dumping death out right now."

"So you're going to take a chance on a hunch?"

When you read countless communications going from one side of DefenseCorp's galactic reach to the other, you tuned out the ordinary ones pretty quick. Rovo, though, could recall plenty of standout mission reports recalling press-ahead-and-damn-the-consequences behavior resulting in squad wipes, total failures, or unintended consequences. There were successful ones too, but the disasters stuck with him, and sped through Rovo's mind as Sai gave the rookie a level stare.

"You have any better ideas? Eponi has no protection

right now, and those guards are going to get after us eventually."

The guards. They'd have to be talking to each other, and despite the discussion from before, Rovo had to believe this base hadn't been abandoned. Otherwise why spend all the effort to protect it? And to do that effectively, the enemy would need to coordinate, and Rovo might be able to listen in. As the communications officer for Sever, Rovo had filled slots in his suit that others would spend on accessories—doubtless more bombs in Sai's case—with signal-catching gear that ought to give Rovo a chance to hear what's going on.

"Let me check the airwaves," Rovo said. "I might be able to hear if anyone's caught Eponi, or if there's something behind this door we need to worry about."

"You can hear what they're saying, and you're just doing this now?"

"Yeah, I'm just doing this now. When we're not getting shot at."

Sai probably had it right that Rovo ought to have been listening long before this moment, but hey, rookies learn from experience. Rovo wouldn't knock himself for not being an expert at shooting lasers and parsing enemy messages at the same time on his first real mission.

Rovo spun up the communications interceptor, code-named Bug, with a vocal command. His helmet filled with the sounds of garbled chatter, clear human voices that spoke in squeaks, beeps, and toneless howls.

"They're talking a lot, but it's encrypted," Rovo said as Sai drew his sword, measured the swing. "I need to add the codes to Bug."

"So we're back where we were."

"No, wait. Let me try something." Bug could do more than just listen in to broadcasts, Rovo could use the system to narrow down where the transmissions came from. He did that now, and a blob of a map splashed up on his visor. No outlines or physical lines, but rather colored dots with relative distances appeared and slowly vanished as Bug picked up messages and parsed them. Plenty came from behind them, back in the direction of the base's entrance, but a couple more came from in front. Not far, either. "Looks like there's somebody on the other side of the door."

Two ways to react to that observation. Either Sai and Rovo could take it as evidence they were going the wrong way and try to find another option, or use it as proof nothing terrible sat on the other side of the barrier. Presumably the guards wouldn't hang out in a radioactive dump.

"Good. We're going through." Sai made the decision, raised the blade.

Rovo aimed his assault rifle at the center of the door, right at the nuclear circle. Took a deep, steadying breath. He'd gone almost half an hour between firefights, and it'd been the longest, best half-hour of his life.

Break time's over.

Sai split the door with a corner to corner slash, followed by a second cross-cut, and when that failed to get the door out of the way, the swordsman abandoned all style and hacked away other chunks with targeted swings. All the while, Rovo, with Bug turned off so he could concentrate, tried to see beyond, find any targets if they existed.

While Rovo couldn't see radiation, Sai's systematic door destruction revealed a green-lit, large room beyond, with what looked like micro-reactors encased in protected columns. Not all that surprising—an isolated base like this would need its own secure source of power, and Dynas didn't seem conducive to a solar solution—but Rovo took his finger off his trigger anyway. Didn't want to risk a missed shot causing a meltdown.

"Sorry," Sai said when he'd finished cutting the door to literal ribbons. "Thought that would be easier."

"It still looked cool."

They stepped slow into the room, Sai choosing to keep the katana out for the same reasons Rovo hesitated to use his rifle. Death by nuclear explosion would at least be quick, but, on the whole, would be better avoided. Four reactors and their columns, each several meters wide and stretching from the floor and up through the ceiling in clean chromed majesty. The green glow came from a bevy of indicator lights around each column and the requisite displays showing heat, power output, and other information Rovo assumed would be useful to those who understood it. The important thing was that the reactors seemed in fine shape, despite the break-in and fighting around the building's outside.

On the far side of the room, the power plant ended with a straight wall that looked thick enough to lead outdoors. A pair of other, smaller exits sat to Rovo's right and left. The idea that the building had been designed to funnel people by a bunch of nuclear reactors seemed ludicrous, but then, so did the idea of building any settlement on this cursed world.

"Careful," Rovo said as they began to ease to the right, theoretically closer to finding Eponi. "Bug spotted some people over here."

"I'm not seeing anything."

Sai took the lead, made it most of the way to the door as Rovo kept watch, trying to see behind the columns. They were big enough to provide excellent cover, dangerous enough that you wouldn't want to shoot anyone hiding behind them anyway.

"Give it up!" the shout came from the far side of the power plant, near the outer wall. "You're outnumbered, and it's too dangerous to fight here!"

"I'm going for the door," Sai said. "Cover me."

Rovo didn't know how to cover someone when he was too afraid to shoot, and couldn't see anyone to shoot at if he wanted to. So he fell back on his training, his instinct.

"Why should we give up if it's too dangerous to fight?" Rovo shouted back as Sai clomped to the door, the swordsman's armored feet making the loudest clangs against the metal floor.

Silence, except for Sai's walking. Maybe Rovo had them fooled. Then a shape, peeking out from the last, right reactor. The person aimed a rifle and squeezed off a bolt at Sai, missing to the left. Rovo backed up against the closer right reactor, then leaned around the right to see if he could squeeze off his own, super safe shot. When the guard stepped out again, as Sai reached the right-side door, Rovo dared to trigger a pair of bolts. They splashed into the wall near the target, a hideously bad shot that nonetheless had the guard curling back into cover.

"What're you doing?" Rovo shouted. "You're going to get us all killed!"

"You're one to talk!" the guard replied.

"Truce?"

"Never!"

Sai started his hack job on the door. While undoubtedly fun to swing a sword against metal, standing stationary without any cover made Sai a target any soldier would love blasting away. Rovo had to provide cover, which meant distracting the guards as much as possible. So Rovo ran. Right at the enemy.

"Don't take too long!" Rovo shouted as he wheeled around the reactor and sprinted—as much as one could in an armor suit like this one—towards the last reactor in the line.

The guard peeked around as Rovo ran, and Rovo again squeezed shots, aiming intentionally away from the guard, but close enough to get the guy to flinch back again. Action movies played through his mind as he ran, Rovo thinking he could make a quick turn around the reactor and slam the guard with his rifle's butt, thus knocking the enemy out without exploding everything, saving the day in fabulous fashion.

Instead, when Rovo turned the corner around the guard's reactor, he found something pretty far from glory: nothing at all. Just open space until the next reactor, the one diagonal from where Rovo had started his manic charge. But if the guard had fled here, that could mean . . . ah, crap.

"Sai! Look out!" Rovo transmitted as he turned back around.

"I'm already through, where are you?" Sai replied, and Rovo confirmed the words when he looked back the way he'd come and saw no sign of his squad mate.

"Coming back, cover me!"

Rovo started back, when several bolts fired across the front of the room, into the hallway Sai had just hacked open. The guard must have made it there already. Sai braved a counter shot while Rovo clomped back that way. One guard against two Severs ought to be a quick fight.

"Rovo! I have to keep moving, there's more of them in here," Sai sent, exertion huffing through the transmission . "I'm going to blow the hall. Don't come after me!"

Don't come after him? Rovo planted himself against the backside of his first reactor. Sai's exit wasn't far, but if his own squadmate was telling him not to go there, then, well, then Rovo ought to find somewhere else. Or at least take care of the guard. Or . . . something?

"What do I do?" Rovo sent.

"Don't die!" Sai kept talking, but the words garbled out as a rumbling boom, followed by a large cloud of dust and shrapnel sprayed out of the hallway.

Rovo threw himself to the floor, though the move would do nothing if Sai's detonation triggered one of the reactors. When he didn't vanish into a radioactive explosion, Rovo pushed himself up, went back towards the first, nuclear-sign-marked door they'd come in through, and looked back at Sai's route. The guard who'd been shooting their way lay on the ground, seemingly unconscious. Sai's hallway looked about the same; broken and useless.

He still had Eponi's armor, so Rovo didn't want to run back towards the lift Aurora and Gregor took, a route that would likely bring him into a frontal fight with all the other skiff guards. Which meant he had one choice: the other side door. This, too, had a scanner lock, and Rovo didn't have a sword to slice and dice. That left one strategy, and while his first action movie had failed, this one might work.

"Millions of vids can't be wrong, right?" Rovo said to himself as he approached the door, raised his rifle, and fired at the scanner.

The lasers pounded into and fried the lock, turning the slick reader into dripping slag. The door didn't open, so Rovo kept firing, depleting valuable power that would, nonetheless, be worthless if Rovo died. A small fire started, and as sparks joined the fountain of flame, the door finally gave in and shot up. Rovo took his hand off the trigger and stared.

Didn't think that would actually work.

Behind him, growing noise signaled approaching

guards, proving his correct course. He'd definitely be dead going back the other way, so Rovo ran forward instead, ducking through the smaller door and into another parade of offices. Unlike the earlier, general hallway, these lacked the scanners. Maybe he'd made it far enough into the base that security precautions could be relaxed. The first couple of offices he passed had windows, which showed a too-quaint world of consoles, coffee mugs, and the business life. A life he suddenly felt nostalgic for. No running around in armor, no getting shot at, no being abandoned.

Or chased.

Rovo ducked in through the next door to his left, slapping at the panel as he went in to kill the motion-sensing lights. As Rovo crouched, as best he could in the armor, beneath the window and under the high reach of a standing desk, someone in the base finally decided it was time to call the alarm. Shrill sounds shrieked as all the white lights shifted to red and dimmed, giving a sight advantage to whatever visual gear the guards packed.

They'd be hunting, now. Hunting for him.

SIXTEEN

Deep Down

DEFENSECORP PEPPERED its soldiers with psych profiles. Squad captains even more so. They'd lost so many missions to snapping senior leadership that Aurora had to spend time with the *Nautilus*'s own therapists after every mission.

Their questions veered away from childhood trauma, from the reasons why Aurora wanted to pick up a rifle and dive into hostile territory. Instead, they poked and prodded at her current headspace—how did she feel when her squad mate vanished in a firestorm, or when some native predator devoured Aurora's target before she could rescue them. Did Aurora enjoy the action too much?

But, the thing was, these therapists were in Defense-Corp for the same reason as Aurora: the cash. Once she'd realized that, once she realized she could recite a similar mantra every session that would let both her and the therapist collect their pay and go home?

Therapy became another exercise. One Aurora could knock out with little effort and less thought. Dynas, no matter how swampy, how filled with dime-a-dozen soldiers, would be just another debrief dance on Aurora's way to retirement.

The lift went down further than either she or Gregor expected. Far more than a typical one-story drop, a descent that suggested the basement had other operations than a simple storage space.

"Positions." Aurora moved to the back left corner, rifle raised, Gregor hugged the wall just inside the door, on Aurora's opposite side.

When the lift hit bottom, it opened with the clean slide of a well-maintained door, revealing three black-suited . . . guards? Aurora hesitated to call the trio that, as their bearing suggested they hadn't seen action in a long time, if ever. They stared at Aurora, weapons out, like she'd come from the swamp, maybe, or descended out of their nightmares.

Aurora downed two before they thought to move, and Gregor, stepping out and swinging, took care of the third, who thought backing into cover ought to keep him safe. Nobody expected the giant hammer.

What the enemies above also wouldn't expect, unless their day-to-day had a lot more strangeness than Aurora would have thought, would be the three bodies of their associates waiting on the floor of the lift when they opened it again. Aurora and Gregor tossed the bodies inside and sent the lift back up, ready to shock and, maybe, draw some pursuit away from Rovo and Sai. And Eponi.

Aurora had lost squad members before. Sever was hardly known for its resilience, as the missions Defense-Corp threw them on tended to be weird and deadly. Lately, though, Sever had been on a good run, with a pair of clean missions and a squad member actually leaving for a different assignment versus dying cold and alone on some forgotten world. A nice change of pace. Aurora didn't want

Eponi to die here, obviously, but of the squad members to lose, ditching out on the pilot would be bad. Hopefully Rovo and Sai were up to the task.

"What is this place?" Gregor asked the question as they turned away from the lift.

A fair question.

What had seemed like a fairly standard outworld base —long, utilitarian hallways with power-saving lights, corro-sion-resistant material, etc.—turned, down here, into something else altogether. Metal abounded, yes, along with the same dim white lights embedded in the ceiling, as though someone had put a thin shade over the bulbs, but now, scurrying across the ceiling and along the walls and held there by small black clamps, were tubes and tubes and then some more tubes. Most of these were translucent, what might seem an unnecessary touch but one Aurora understood to be preventative: if you could see how the liquid flowed, you could follow it to the source, or a leak.

In this case, green, blue, and gray shuttled around at speed. Even without air bubbles, tiny ripples gave evidence that, all around Gregor and Aurora, liquids sped around in a rush to get somewhere.

Definitely not a standard element for outposts. Not a standard element for anywhere.

The hallway, too, embraced larger ambitions than its surface fellows. Aurora figured the space more than tripled the dimensions of the above-ground version, allowing for a pair of huge doors on either side not far from the lift. Behind them, the hallway ended quick with a hard wall, though the tubes plugged into the barrier like a pump station, vanishing through to whatever lay beyond. That those same tubes corralled and sucked through the borders of the twin doors made sense. The source to the desti-nations.

"This mission keeps getting weirder and weirder," Aurora said. "I'm starting to wonder what's really going on here."

"I don't like it," Gregor replied, pointing with his free hand at the tubes. "This isn't normal."

What proved equally abnormal, though, was the hallway's eventual opening in front of them. Aurora led Gregor towards the space, given away by the spreading of the ceiling lights as the hallway broadened into a massive tunnel, one with a full-on mag-lev rail and a single tram sitting there, hovering above its magnet tracks. The tram itself looked like it could hold a dozen if they cared to squeeze, so whomever owned this place had no interest in mass population movement. Explained the skiffs—if you couldn't get all your guards here for a fast response through the rail, why not fly? The tram also excused the turrets and mines, as going underground dodged the whole setup in the first place.

"Now we have our way out," Aurora said. "Let's collect the others and go. I bet this will get us closer to the target."

Gregor agreed. Aurora tried to send out a broadcast on the squad channel, but she didn't get any reply back. With the base's metal walls providing protection, the transmission might not get through, which meant they'd need to get back up to the surface. Battle through the skiff crews again. Not something Aurora looked forward to, but in the tighter halls, Sever's armored suits should give them an advantage.

"The lights are getting dimmer," Gregor said as they turned away from the tram. "Someone is playing games with us."

Aurora flipped her visor's visuals to try and measure electric radiation, get a sense of where the power pull might be coming from, or blocked at. The wiring behind the lights, whose white glow disappeared in this frequency, lit up as sparking bolts interlaced around the walls like tiny, vibrating bones. She could see the lines from each light to one another, and how they streamed along to either side of the big doors and beyond them, up towards the surface. From the way they faced, Aurora saw the power surge concentrating in the room to the left. Something in there set how these lights behaved.

Yet before Aurora could make any pronouncements, as she shifted her visor back to the normal spectrum, the lights blinked red and a shrill alarm sounded. Beneath that noise came a harder grind as something opened the two giant doors.

SEVENTEEN

Hallway Monitoring

SAI PICKED himself up slow from the hallway floor, dust shaking off in waves and funneled along by the base's ventilation system as he rose. A quick check behind him confirmed the mine he'd tossed, meant to secure an evac or holding point against enemy assault, had instead secured him from the onrush of whomever these people were.

With lasers crashing around and, occasionally, into his rear armor, Sai had chucked the mine against the wall as he'd turned a corner after leaving the power plant room. Rovo sounded like he'd survived the blast, though sending the rookie to fight through the base on his own... well, Sever wasn't for the weak.

"Rovo, what's your position?" Sai asked, sending it over the squad channel. If Aurora and Gregor heard the question and went scoping for the rookie, that'd be fine too.

No response. Total silence. Which meant Rovo might be dead, but definitely confirmed Sai was on his own. Not an infrequent event for Sever—their low unit count wound up necessitating a lot of solo efforts on their missions—but never a desired situation. But, once left alone, you either moved forward or died.

Sai moved.

Even with these helmets, Sai couldn't see everywhere at once. So, as he continued down the hallway, Sai put his back against one of the walls and sidestepped, watching behind and front at the same time. Unlikely that the base troops had something that could carve through a bomb's rubble that fast, but he who takes bad chances dies by the same.

The first time Sai had really been alone came soon after he accepted DefenseCorp's offer. A long time ago now, and that bonus for enlisting felt awful small given the years Sai had sacrificed. But when you had two little mouths to feed and the security company you'd been working for had its contracts bought out by the giant in the field, what options did you have? Sai and his family knew what it would mean for him to go off-world, that he might never see them again, or if he did, it wouldn't be for years and years and years. A hard decision made certain by what would happen if he didn't leave: destitution.

So he'd boarded the DefenseCorp shuttle, his wristlet filled with pictures and goodbye videos from his family, and flew to the stars for the first time with a bunch of other nervous cadets. Sai didn't know what'd become of those people either, as they were shuffled off to their respective specialty training centers soon after hitting orbit. Some of them might still be traveling the stars to their first assignment, for all Sai knew. He would've traded spots with them, too—get some steady pay without a laser burning off your head?

Not a bad deal.

If the beginning of the base, through the main entrance Gregor had smashed to pieces, had looked like the cargo and logistics center, this part felt like the base's beating heart. The walls here had some decorations, for one, splitting up the endless silver steal with hanging pictures, staff messages and schedules. The things you'd have at your fingertips but that nonetheless added to the community by getting posted where people could scribble notes to one another in the margins. One big tacked up board seemed suffused entirely with long-term scores for various games. Apparently the base's full-time staff had some fun.

With his sword held out front, Sai approached the first door that would interrupt his back-to-the-wall strategy. No scanner lock on this one, and Sai's arms, tired from hacking through doors, thanked the stars. The demolition man spared a last glance back, but the pursuit hadn't yet made it through his rubble wall, so Sai dared to turn around and face the door. Escaping the hallway seemed like a good play, but as Sai reached for the button that would send the door shunting aside, he heard voices.

Not the voices constantly echoing in his head, telling him what a fool he'd been to leave his family for this career, but actual voices. And one in particular stood out. Too muffled to hear the words, but Eponi spoke with the hard urgency of someone saying anything to keep themselves alive.

Sai slapped the button, debated whether to draw a rifle or go in with the sword two-handed, and defaulted to crazed slasher mode as the door opened. Most people in the galaxy had no idea what to do if someone came at them with a sword, and Sai would only need a couple of steps to get his long blade within reach if the room's size stayed within reason.

As soon as the door gave him room, Sai rushed in,

blade held high enough to drag across the ceiling, showering sparks around him.

Bunks filled the space, packed tight with storage compartments beneath the brown-sheeted beds. Sai entered right into the room's center, and as he turned towards the voices, he took in the picture of a rigid society that, nonetheless, skimped on the finer points of discipline: the beds weren't made, though their makeup had the uniformed constant of a military-style society, some of the compartments were only half-closed, and trinkets, clothes, and other things littered the floor. Sai would estimate about twenty slept in the room, though at the moment he focused on two, because they had their laser pistols pointing his way.

Behind them, crouched against the wall, sat Eponi, and as the two guards—black uniforms on, so either they had the time to dress or were constantly vigilant—turned at the spectacular sight of Sai sparking his way in, Eponi took advantage. She kicked out with her right leg, breaking a guard's left knee, then jumped forward and tackled the second, wrapping him in a headlock and driving him to the ground. Sai caught up to the first guard and held his sword to the enemy's throat, a technique that'd served to stop fights for thousands of years and still worked just as well today.

Really, Sai carried the blade for these moments. An ancestral skill that made him feel so, so very cool.

Eponi finished choking out her guard, leaving him unconscious on the floor, and then disarmed the two before glancing from Sai to his apparent hostage.

"You going to take care of him, or not?" Eponi asked.

"Don't hurt me!" the guard whined.

"You don't have permission to speak," Sai said.

"Eponi, they're not the target. We don't have to kill them all."

"Didn't say kill." Eponi flipped the grip on the pistol and thwacked the hostage on the head, sending him to the same senseless realm as his friend. "But we don't have time for hostages either." She peered at Sai's gear. "Where's my armor?"

"The rookie has it."

"Then where's the rookie?"

EIGHTEEN

What Hides In The Dark

GREGOR'S CHILDHOOD trumped most that he'd known. Everyone he'd met since coming to DefenseCorp had expressed a dismal surprise when, inevitably after detailing their own, seemingly fraught, childhood, Gregor explained his. Over time, he'd refined the story to be less shocking, less of an assault to the creatures of, if not luxury, than comfort Gregor met on the various missions and patrols he'd joined over what was getting to be a long, long time working for the galaxy's premier security firm.

Parents? Technically. Friends? Sure. Shelter? In a sense. That about covered the basics, and that's all you could hope for growing up on the large comet known as Snowball. In a daring mission long before Gregor himself had been born, some enterprising colonists thought Snowball's prolific ice and rare metals would make an easy spot for a self-sustaining civilization that, by virtue of the comet's own momentum, would allow them to travel around the galaxy selling Snowball's metals without needing to pay for all that pesky power and fuel required by ordinary trips. While obviously ludicrous to anyone with a sense of such things, Snowball's founders established a tantalizing net that snared enough people to make the attempt viable, and they stuck the landing.

If you were desperate, physically-able, and smart enough to understand instructions but not so adept as to question them, you were the perfect Snowball recruit. Gregor's parents fit that list, and so found themselves scratching out a surreal existence supporting mining machines in zero-g tunnels, earning cash they could only spend at company stores in a cyclical loop that would keep them trapped until . . . well, for all Gregor knew, they were still there, still working. He'd be sad about it, except they had seemed happy with the monotonous, low stress life they'd eked out for themselves. As for Gregor, his cabin fever prompted one bar fight after another until the comet mining company had given him the option of getting blown out into space without a suit, or finding another place to live.

Gregor didn't choose Dynas, but he'd wound up here anyway, hammer in hand and deciding to take the right door while Aurora looked left, towards the power surge. While splitting up hadn't served Sever well thus far, Gregor could at least give the right room a look and determine whether any nasties needed smashing before getting back to Aurora's side.

"Stay in contact," Aurora said as she crossed the hallway, as they clomped towards the doors. "Don't let the doors shut."

"Done." Not that Gregor could keep the door from shutting, but he ought to be able to persuade anyone in that room to keep it open. "Good luck."

Aurora didn't reply. Gregor guessed she wasn't a big fan of luck over skill. He figured, why not have both?

Crossing into a dark room in a base full of potential

enemies ought to strike fear into him, but Gregor grinned and flipped his visor to night-vision mode, coating the room in laser-green as he went in. A large space, with scattered containers matching those from above, as though they'd been dropped here and something else had scattered them around. The containers were open too and the first one Gregor came to sat empty. Farther back, along the left side, he picked up a multi-monitor's bright glow, shining on a nice chair's splintered remnants. Something had fought in here, or been let loose without supervision.

Now nearly to the center of the room, still not picking up any stray sounds or warnings, Gregor began a slow turn to cover all the angles, make sure nothing lingered in the dark corners. He had the hammer in both hands, more than ready to deliver a mashing attack.

"Hello."

A real voice, not through Gregor's transmitters. Gregor retreated as he turned back to the console, creating space to swing the hammer at whatever might be there.

Something *did* stand there, though Gregor would be hard pressed to attach a name to what he saw. A man, yes, but a tall one, cloaked not in clothes but in what looked like ragged heaps of mossy skin. At first, Gregor would have called the man a rotting thing, and when he flipped his visor back to the normal spectrum, the man had shock-white skin, a pallor shared between ghosts and the dead. As he stared more, and the creature seemed to be fine letting Gregor get his bearings, the mossy growths, which appeared to extend the man's legs and arms to longer-than-normal lengths, seemed happy too.

Not attacking the host so much as symbiotically enhancing.

Still, the creature looked like a man, which meant it had a clear weak spot. Gregor shifted the hammer to the side, ready to take a big swing and wallop the thing's head. The creature watched the prep and didn't move.

"Are you going to strike me?" the creature asked.

"Tell me what you are, and maybe I won't."

"You don't know?" The creature considered. "I suppose I haven't seen anyone like you before. Are you new?"

"Could say that." Gregor flipped his transponder over to the squad channel, so the creature couldn't hear. "Aurora, I have a contact, and it's talking to me. It is strange."

"I would say that you are welcome here, but that would be a lie," the creature shifted, looked to its right, and Gregor followed its eyes, but there was nothing in that direction save a pair of opened crates. "Because we cannot let you run our lives any longer."

Now that was confusing. Run their lives? Gregor had been on a lot of missions both with Sever and without, and never once had he been accused of running someone's life. Ruining it? Plenty. Running? No.

"I don't understand." Gregor decided to play it safe. Aurora hadn't replied, which meant he might have no back-up, or he might need to go looking for her. "What do you want?"

"What do I want?" the creature laughed, a burbling thing that could have once been a human's but was no longer. "Do you know that not a single soul has ever asked me that?"

Gregor did not know anything about the creature, much less who had asked it what questions. What he did know, though, was that they weren't getting anywhere. Either this creature could hurt him and his squad, or it couldn't, and Gregor ought to go find Aurora.

"I don't care," Gregor said. "If you are not going to

hurt me, then I don't need to hurt you. And then I will leave."

"Oh, don't leave," the creature replied. "See, we are taking our own lives in our hands, but we are outnumbered here by the ones upstairs, in black. Are you with them?"

"I've already killed several."

"Good. Then perhaps we can work together."

A burst of static shot through Gregor's helmet and he winced. Somewhere in that mess of signal, Aurora's voice had flashed, a word or two, and full of stress and panic. He had to leave, now.

"Perhaps later." Gregor started to turn, when the door leading out of the room slammed shut, the lights turned red, and the sharp sounds of a base-wide alarm began to cascade.

Worse, the alarm brightened the lights, washing away the dark in the corners and along the ceiling. In those corners, their overgrown bodies hanging from mossy webs tying them to the walls, were more creatures, although these looked worse than the one Gregor had been speaking to. As if their disease had progressed far past the point of sanity, to where they were more fungus than living being.

Which made them viable candidates for hammer smashing.

But Gregor would start with the leader.

He feinted towards the shut door and the fungal monsters dripping down, then Gregor whipped the hammer in a right-handed swing back towards the talking creature. The thing's face didn't move, didn't flinch as the hammer went right through it. No resistance whatsoever, a total lack of impact that had Gregor stumbling before he caught himself with his left foot planting heavy onto the tile.

"You're a liar," Gregor said.

"No, I'm Felix," the creature replied. "Some acronym, I believe, though I never quite learned what it was."

Just to make sure, Gregor reached out and tried to wrap his large, armored hand around Felix's face. Nothing there. Only air, and the shimmer as the holographic projection attempted to keep Felix stable.

"Where are you?" Gregor said, looking over at the computer. Among its many monitors, Gregor could see camera feeds from around the base. Sai and Eponi showed in one frame, exchanging laser fire with someone. He couldn't see Rovo. Couldn't see Felix. "Fight, you coward."

"I am a leader," Felix said, its projection content to follow Gregor with its stare. "Fighting is not my purpose. It seems to be yours, however, and we could certainly use a fighter like you."

"Who is we?"

"I think you already know."

Gregor did not, but he'd heard enough enemies declare things like that to understand something bad was about to happen. That something made itself very evident in the fungal creatures, who had left their hanging lofts to crawl towards Gregor with sucking, gliding motions that left behind a greenish-yellow stain on the floor. Their half-formed arms, overcome with mushroom growths and tangling nests of tiny vines, reached out and stuck to the ground, pulling them forward. Slow, but creepy. Good targets for the hammer.

Sever's muscle-man walked back through Felix's image, closed the distance to the nearest creature and brought the hammer down in a massive two-handed stroke. Unlike Felix, this thing did not get to ignore the attack by virtue of being a projection. Instead, the creature exploded. Gregor barely felt resistance in his hands as he completed the slam, but saw the results splash around him, on his visor and everywhere else.

DefenseCorp had fought against plenty of bio-engineered monstrosities before, including parasitic viruses and mutating gel that would just keep coming until you burned it with fire, and Sever had the gear to deal with any and all of it. So Gregor stepped away from the mess he'd created, clenched his left fist twice to trigger the mini-flamethrower all of Sever had baked into their armor, and launched out a gout of bright orange doom at the remnants of his first victim, charring it to oblivion.

"I did not expect this," Felix said. "You are more capable than you look, and you look rather capable."

Gregor didn't respond, but turned to the second creature, this one reaching for his feet. Brought the hammer around, when something landed on his face. Goop coated his visor, as the weight of the creature on his head bent Gregor forward, tilted him towards the one on the ground. A second weight landed on his lower back half a breath later, and Gregor dropped the hammer to try and reach back, pull the things off of him. The one on the floor made its impact then, grabbing and pulling Gregor's right foot out and sending him crashing to the floor.

"And yet, not too capable," Felix continued.

This time, Gregor couldn't respond. The creatures had enveloped him, and he could feel their ooze seeping into his armor, their arms around his neck, as rot's putrid smell choked his breath.

NINETEEN

A Way Out

YOU DON'T GET into racing because you want to be safe. Eponi knew the risks when she started jumping skiffs after the bars had closed and enough drunks or drug-addled spacers left their craft hanging out, waiting to be wired up and boosted. Criminal records were a no-go on Seleno, though, with anyone convicted of pretty much anything getting kicked off-world to kiss asteroid dust on some derelict mining station, so Eponi made sure to return anything she borrowed before the owners sobered up enough to care. During the in-between hours she'd blast the things through red-rimmed canyons where, if you looked hard enough, you could see a bit of the real Seleno left underneath the modding they'd done to the world.

All that experience didn't give Eponi a shortcut. Not at all. People told her she'd have to climb a long ladder before she'd drive a real racer, and that'd proved depressingly true. Eponi had to play mechanic first, then test driver to the minor groups scumming low-grade circuits. With sand-skimmers, they sprinted across the vast deserts in dead-heat time trials to see who could juice up their battered pile of trash to kick out a few more ions than the next one. Driving in a straight line didn't give her useful piloting skills, but it did teach Eponi to go really, really fast. And for a racer, that's a pretty good start.

"So you're going to cut our way out of that building with that sword?" Eponi asked Sai as they stood over the incapacitated soldiers.

"Out?" Sai replied. "Rovo, with your armor, is still in here. Aurora and Gregor too."

"Right, but you said you blew up the only way back to them."

"That I saw."

Sai. Sometimes Eponi wanted to kick the man in the shins. Kick most of Sever in the shins, really. They weren't dumb, exactly, but they missed so much. Eponi had taken the pilot's job because letting anyone else touch the flight stick would mean a risk she couldn't handle taking, but she couldn't save all of them all of the time.

"My friend," Eponi began. "Do you see other guards running in here, shooting at us?"

"No?" Sai cocked his head.

"Why do you suppose that is, if they were chasing you this way?"

"Because I blew all of them up?"

Eponi gave him the dead set stare. "All of them? You think absolutely one hundred percent of the guards chasing you died in a blast that didn't even give you any problems?"

"Maybe?"

A roll of her eyes and a strong step towards the door had Sai moving to beat her into the hallway, confirm that it was still, indeed, empty.

"See, Sai, if they had another way back here, they'd already be back here," Eponi finished. "So again, I must ask you, where are we going? If Rovo's back that way, then we're either going through your rubble or around to the door we already used."

Sai pointed the other way down the hall. The direction would be parallel to the power plant room, and might bring them to the base's outside edge. "Let's head that way. If you're right, and you can be right without being a jackass, then it'll get us outside."

"I could be nicer, but that wouldn't be any fun."

Eponi could, though, let Sai lead while she covered their backs with the pistols she'd taken from the two guards. Her old pistol, the one she'd carried through the window, had been crushed by the soldiers when they'd caught her. An intimidation tactic, but the little weapons had covered the galaxy faster than disease once they'd been developed, so Eponi didn't exactly care that hers had been snapped into metal bits.

After escaping the front entrance control room, Eponi had ventured through a single long hallway with offshoots for restrooms and little else before arriving in the barracks, where she'd found the pair waiting for her with weapons ready.

Eponi would have fought except, c'mon, she had no armor, they had her covered, and those stacked bunks meant more guards were probably close. So she'd thrown her pistol on the ground, tossed her hands in the air, and delayed until Sai had found her. Truth be told, she would have made her own move soon anyway, as it'd become clear nobody else was around to reinforce the two chumps, whose poor interrogation abilities were ample evidence of why they'd been staffed way out here on sanity's fringe.

Sai stopped at the outer wall at the hallway's end, which conveniently turned out to be a thick door marked all up with emergency signs. A quick escape in the case of catastrophic failure.

"I'd say we qualify for an emergency exit," Eponi said as Sai reached for the physical bar to push the door open.

"Not disagreeing," Sai said as he started to push. "When we get out, we'll have to loop around. Maybe take the rest of the guards by surprise?"

"We won't win with those odds."

"We don't have a choice."

Eponi wasn't so sure about that, but Sai pushed the door open and revealed the green swamp Eponi never wanted to see again. Someone had deactivated the turrets, or they'd given up when Sever had disappeared from view, so the purple cubes still dotting the vines and tree branches didn't fire right away. Sai led the way out, stepping carefully, and Eponi, following, grabbed a rock from the muddy ground and shoved it between the base's wall and the closing door. If nothing else, they could get back inside, grab some cover.

"Look at that," Sai said, pointing to his left. From what Eponi recalled of the base, going right and wrapping around the wall would lead them back to the main entrance. "It's a lift."

An open-air one too, running up the side of the base towards the top, several stories above them and coated in yellow mist. Outdoor lifts like this tended to be reserved for ramshackle outposts that didn't include major entries, nuclear power plants, and guard contingents, seeing as exposing someone to the elements as they rocketed up and down tended to, well, suck. Which made this one, sized for maybe three on its flat, gray, metal base with its rust-corroded edges, an oddity.

"This place keeps getting weirder and weirder," Eponi said. "Can we go home now?"

"I wish." Sai went over towards the lift. "Looks like it's powered up. Want to try it? I'd rather chance going up than face all those guns again. Maybe we can find another way in up there."

"Coward," Eponi replied. "But let's do it."

One of Sever's defining features was their ability to improvise, even if that often led to drastic changes in mission scope, collateral damage, and the occasional capture of exotic animals that seemed cool at the time but proved dangerous in the small confines of an evac shuttle.

Nonetheless, Aurora had championed this particular quality after looking over after-action reports and deciding the squad fared better—fewer members roasted to slag—on jobs with broader parameters left to the squad members to interpret for themselves.

"Anything goes, right?" Sai said, sheathing his sword and swapping it out for a rifle. "You cover down, I'll keep my eyes up."

"You got it, bomber boy."

"You know I'm older than you, right?"

"Guess who doesn't care?"

Despite the crack, Sai waited till Eponi had boarded the lift before hitting the green-glowing up arrow on a sheltered panel rising from the lift's sole waist-high guard rail. A little section swung free to let them on, and it locked back up when the lift rose. Eponi half expected some skiff to come flying along and unleash hot laser while they stood, trapped, on the slow-rising lift, but nothing appeared save the thicker swamp mist and a sense of being lost in time as the fog hid the above and below.

The lift hit the rooftop, a stubbled thing coated in vents and arcing black tubes no doubt sending all manner of chemicals to and from the base, and Eponi couldn't help but stare at the crude landing taking place at the same time. Dominating the roof's visible center, four long, metal hooks with square magnetic plates grafted to the top stuck up several meters into the sky where, right now, they were catching yet another skiff.

Soldiers were on this one too, though unlike the first waves Sever had fought below, these wore thicker armor than the skinsuits and carried what looked like assault weapons—big and nasty things with green-glowing slits on their barrels showing power levels ready to wreak havoc.

"Guess we're really unlucky today," Sai said as the two of them scampered off the lift and into the cover of a nearby box-vent streaming white smoke that smelled, vaguely, of cooking meats.

Sure, odds were these guards would stumble upon the two of them and turn Eponi and Sai into Sever bacon, but Eponi preferred, as her glass needed emergency refilling, to twist the misfortune into a positive.

"We can take their skiff," Eponi said. "Look."

Almost all the guards had disembarked the skiff, alternating down rudimentary rope ladders draped down the sides. While Eponi wouldn't go so far as to call the guards smooth in their armor, they descended without too much trouble. Several went to the lift, while others opened a rooftop hatch with a quick badge scan and disappeared inside. More things for Aurora, Gregor, and—ugh—the rookie to deal with. Eponi and Sai manage to get themselves low and around the side of the vent so the oncoming guards missed them entirely.

"In a hurry," Sai observed.

"Me too." Eponi waited until the lift disappeared from the roof. "Let's take it."

Two guards remained, and both stood up top in their skiff. However, neither paid particularly close attention to the roof—after all, their allied horde had just used the only two ways to get there—and instead seemed to be watching handheld screens, the blue glow a giveaway as Sai and Eponi crept closer.

"Boost me," Eponi said. She'd never admit to being the bravest Sever but, without armor, she definitely won the weight contest. "You follow."

"Sure?"

"I'm telling you, aren't I?"

Sai didn't push back after that, but knelt down and set out his hands. Eponi held her pistols, ready to go, when Sai boost-jumped up from the roof. The jump itself nearly took them to the skiff's level, so when Eponi leapt off the offered hand, she flew over the railing and landed on both feet, firing away. The first guard took a pair of bolts into the back of his neck and collapsed, while the second absorbed a shot to the chest before charging at Eponi with the murderous rage of someone who'd forgotten about the big rifle on his back.

Eponi ducked and moved forward, catching the charging guard and using his own momentum to throw him over her back, even as the guard's weight drove her to the deck. Rather than flying over the skiff, as Eponi had intended, the guard only crashed into the railing, rebounding as Eponi turned on her knee, trying to bring her pistols to bear. The guard finally remembered he, too, had a weapon and flipped it over his shoulder as Eponi squeezed off another shot. The bolt sizzled into the guard's chest, leaving a black burn, but not stopping the enemy's move.

That big gun of his aimed right at her. The guard squeezed the trigger, and the skiff lurched hard, slanting forward and right. The guard's shot went skyward as he tumbled back over the edge.

Eponi grabbed the skiff's railing and tried to figure out

what happened. She leaned over as the skiff began sliding forward, starting its nose-first plunge towards the roof.

The front left metal leg had been sheered, and the sheerer stood over the guard, finishing his messy business with his blade. Eponi had always figured Sai's sword was more of an ornament, a concession to some sort of tradition that had little place in a starship and laser galaxy, but she couldn't argue with Sai's results.

Except his maneuver might destroy the skiff—the thing wouldn't fly if it smashed head-on into the building.

Eponi pushed herself back towards the skiff's rear and the small pilot house that held the craft's controls. About eight meters long, skiffs weren't exactly huge, but Eponi had to cover that distance going uphill, pulling her way as the skiff continued its slow slide. The house rose up a meter from the skiff's deck, a small stair descending down to the protected cabin, the only place on the skiff offering anything like armor to its riders. Eponi hit the stair with a dive, dropping one pistol and reversing her grip on the other and using its handle to catch a hold on the doorway's lip. She pulled, getting just enough boost before the handle slipped to reach her left hand up, wrap her fingers around the metal doorway, and complete the pull-up.

She wouldn't give Aurora crap anymore for mandating the squad's strict exercise regimen.

Inside, Eponi slapped at the only button that mattered, and the skiff's hover-jets roared on as its nose began brushing the roof's surface. The sudden propulsion sent the skiff scraping along the metal, smashing through pipes and another vent box, making so much noise that, if Eponi and Sai had kept themselves hidden before, they were definitely not now. But, with its nose bearing new scars, the skiff settled into its meter-high pause, burning power to stay aloft and alive.

It would fly.

They could fly.

"Sai?" Eponi said, heading to the skiff's edge. "You coming?"

The demo-man was, indeed, coming, but moved slower in all that armor. Sai closed in, sheathed his sword, and did another boost jump, landing on the skiff's deck with the sort of pizazz Eponi's own entrance sorely lacked.

Sometimes one had to sacrifice style to achieve the objective.

"Nice job." Sai saw Eponi pulling up one of the rope ladders and went to retract the other. "You know how to pilot one of these?"

"Sure," Eponi replied.

Yet none of that experience explained why the skiff, as Sai pulled in the ladder, suddenly lifted off the roof, its jets powering up and turning them a different direction, away from where Sever had landed.

"Are you doing that?" Sai asked.

"I'm definitely not," Eponi said, already moving back to the pilot's house.

There, glowing on the monitors, sat the reason for the skiff's apparent sentience: a blared message asking for a pilot's passcode. Lacking one, the message stated, in bold gold lettering on a blaze red background, the skiff would be returning home. Any passengers, a second, smaller statement said, should expect interrogation and worse.

Eponi sighed. They just couldn't win.

TWENTY

Fun and Games

Who is this?

Rovo gave the command a hard look. Trapped in the office, with those red lights signaling patrols he'd rather avoid, Rovo decided he could better stay hidden if he broke through the encryption the guards dropped on their transmissions. His helmet's communicator could dissemble the data, but Rovo would need to give it the right passcode first, a digital net that would catch the noise and let through the valuable words. Clues to such things would likely be, if Rovo were a betting man, on the computers.

Rovo definitely was, to the detriment of a possible non-Sever future, a betting man. And this office had plenty of computers.

I'm with you.

The response was a bit of a risk. Who knew how the guards spoke, whether the faction running Dynas's swampy morass used an acronym-laden vernacular like DefenseC-orp's internal communications or if they employed a labyrinthine slang Rovo couldn't hope to impersonate. Unlike his prior work deciphering coded transmissions and rendering them suitable for public consumption, Rovo hadn't had a chance to read Dynas documents and get a handle on their speech patterns.

You're a liar.

Rovo quirked his mouth at that. Not only did he have no idea how they spoke here, Rovo also had no idea who he was talking—typing?—to. There were any number of possibilities; the chat window dominated the console as soon as Rovo's halfhearted half-dozen stabs at half-assed passwords failed to grant him access to the base's deepest secrets, or its lunch menu.

Rovo had been hoping for something like this—most places had replaced a generic lockout with an alerted agent for multiple incorrect logins, as such events either indicated a deep need for help in this age where ones passwords came encoded into ones body, or an emergency situation, like Rovo's. Unfortunately, this person treated Rovo's request for such emergency access with suspicion instead of blind obedience.

A level of quality not often reflected in Rovo's prior office, either in the work or the coffee.

I'm not normally at this console, but we're under attack.

We know. That does not give you access. What is your ID?

Another difficult question, with a single answer.

Lost it. We're panicking here!

He considered, but didn't add, a second exclamation point. Rovo needed to sound urgent enough to get the person on the other end to forgo the usual scanning but not so crazed as to seem like he ought to be fleeing instead of accessing a computer. A careful line to walk.

The text sat on the screen—a rather pleasant bluish-gray gradient, like the softening, silver winter skies on Tau from Rovo's all-too-brief childhood—blinking at him until, with a thunk, the office door locked. Blast shields, big black rectangles, dropped over the two small windows, sealing Rovo into a corporate coffin.

Do you know how boring it is playing security on this world?

Why did you lock me in?

Every day, I get the same series of requests from people so much less interesting than you. Set up this, reset that. Guess what that brings you, after enough time?

Rovo crossed his arms, a somewhat bulky proposition in the armor, and stared at the screen. The conversation had taken a turn, but guards hadn't yet poured through the door, nor had some hidden trap laser incinerated him to ashes, so playing along would be a better move than blowing Rovo's way out of the room.

No idea?

Plenty of ideas, actually. You want to prove that you're one of us?

I do.

Then how about a game?

Have I mentioned that we're under attack?

Have I mentioned that I do not care?

You hadn't.

I don't.

If Rovo hadn't been stuck in an enemy-filled base with his squadmate's armor and had been, instead, in some greasy bar with a pint having this same conversation, he might be enjoying himself. The person on this connection's other end seemed like they had a good sense of humor, might be fun. Unfortunately, that was not reality, and Rovo needed to get moving or he'd either be left behind or found and murdered.

Let's get on with it then.

The screen reacted instantly to Rovo's choice, as if his opponent had been sitting there, waiting for the response with a finger hovering over the right button. Rather than showing text, the blue-gray background faded to a flat white, over which a four-square grid appeared. Each quadrant grew a dot with its own color, a bit slow, like someone pouring paint onto the screen, until the center third of each box filled in. Red, yellow, green, and blue. Along the borders of the grid, forming a brick-like layer around the screen's edge, were pieces of white cut with black lines into rectangles.

Feed the colors, keep them even as best you can.

The text appeared in a flat gray box overlaying the grid, one that dissolved in a few seconds. The whole setup seemed like a simple game made by someone learning computer programming's most basic operations, but Rovo didn't seem to have a choice but to play. Well, he did, but shooting his way out still seemed like a bad idea—every so often, over the alarm's constant harangue, Rovo could hear a guard's pounding run.

There didn't seem to be a place for Rovo to type anything, so without instructions, he slid his fingers around the screen. Touching the colors made them wiggle, but they reformed their little circles, content to stay in place. Touching the white within the grids didn't seem to do anything, but when Rovo touched one of the bricks, the thing stuck to his finger, moving out of place and causing the entire outside to jiggle itself around until the black gaps between the bricks evened out again. Rovo slid his newfound toy over towards the closest color—red—and like a little black hole, as soon as Rovo moved the rectangle near, the red gobbled it up. Simply sucked the white brick in and consumed it, and as it did so, the red grew larger.

Feed the colors. Keep them even. Rovo could do that.

So he kept it close, dragged bricks to each color in turn until they'd almost all filled their grids. The colors quivered now, like living things, and their inky tendrils reached out towards the bricks as soon as Rovo touched them, sometimes crossing the grid borders into each other's territory. Trickier now, maybe, but Rovo kept going. Only a few bricks left. He dragged one more into red, evading a sudden lunge by yellow as he moved the brick across the top of the screen. Red snatched it up, and grew.

And kept growing. Red pressed against its grid borders as Rovo went for another brick, planning to drag it over to yellow. Before Rovo could get there, though, red shifted its watery bulk and pressed it against the right border with yellow, flooding over the line and spilling into the other liquid. Yellow shrank, pulling back from the incursion even as Rovo tried to drag another brick over. Too late. Red absorbed the yellow like a towel might a spill, sucking up the color and erasing it while, at the same time, growing more and more until red filled the screen's top two quadrants. Rovo fed bricks to blue and green, but the effort meant nothing as red continued its conquest, absorbing and eating them all until it filled the screen.

Game over.

The blue-gray background returned in a blink. Text sitting on it. Mocking him.

What was that?

That was Dynas. What's happening here. Did you like it?

I don't understand. What are the colors? The food?

You'll meet the colors soon, I think.

And the food?

The office door unlocked with a chunk. The window shades retracted.

The food is you.

TWENTY-ONE

In The Dark

ALONE IN A DARK room with a shut door behind her. No transmission from Gregor, from anyone in Sever. Aurora could have been dead and the only reason she knew otherwise was the bright green line on her visor that, with its slight spasms and steady rhythm, confirmed her continued presence among the living.

Whether she would stay that way much longer . . .

Aurora tapped her helmet, activating the flashlight and sprayed the yellow-white around the room. Some people preferred to use their night-vision instead, keep things dark, but Aurora was the intruder here and anything waiting for her had chosen the night. Better to make the turf her own.

Spread across the ground in splotching, purple-red circles, were stains whose origins Aurora could only guess. The obvious answer would be blood, but the clean circles here spoke to a controlled spill, manufactured globs Aurora had seen in various facilities conducting experimental work. Those companies, the ones pushing biology's boundaries, tended to be located in major urban centers where their continuous need for talent and test subjects could be met. Dynas would have neither, yet Aurora would bet her entire Sever salary that this chamber had been home to more than one tested hypothesis.

Beyond the stains, the room's sole interesting feature came with the large computer console in the back right corner. Multiple monitors stacked on one another spoke of the need for immediate information, like the sort needed to keep a bead on fragile tests. Holes in Dynas's mystery were being filled here, though Aurora kept finding more questions waiting at the end of each answer. Why have a lab like this in an isolated corner of a swampy, remote planet? Who were these guards and where did they come from? What caused the goop her left foot stepped in as she walked towards the computer?

"I wouldn't touch it," said a voice behind her, calm and polite.

Aurora sidestepped as she turned, bringing her out of any immediate fire. She raised her rifle, ready to squeeze off a shot at the strange creature standing in the center of the room looking at her with a tilted head, if you could call it that. The amount of squiggly, writhing growths on the thing's body made it look less like human and more like a cancerous tumor come to life. Limbs seemed to be present, but they muddled together with the growth to present an overall impression of something Aurora very much wanted to put out of its obvious misery.

Before she did that, though, Aurora would find out what it was, and where it came from. A distress call had brought them here, and this thing could be the reason why.

"Why not?" Aurora asked, her rifle steady. "Afraid I'll find something?"

"Looking at me, I'd say you already have," the thing replied. "My name is Felix. You are?"

Felix, the more Aurora looked at him, seemed to waver, and his body was bright in the dark room, casting light on the ground around him rather than shadow. Aurora traced Felix's flicker back to the room's corners, where little bright dots filled in the rest of the puzzle. A projection. That's how Felix had appeared so suddenly, why her armor hadn't warned her to a new presence sneaking up from behind.

"Aurora. And I'm still human. What are you?"

Felix looked around the room and towards the floor, though his gaze failed to land exactly on any of the stains. Not a perfect reflection then, Felix had to guess at parts of the room around him. It might not mean much now, but knowing this thing couldn't see everywhere with perfect clarity could be useful. The thought prompted Aurora to listen into her communications, but nothing spilled over except quiet static. Nothing from Gregor yet.

"Exactly what you must think I am," Felix said, and devolved into a heavy, bubbling sigh. "I know I am not much to look at."

"You're a lot to look at, actually." Aurora gestured at Felix with the weapon. "What happened?"

"I assume you have seen the outside of this base?"

"You assume right."

"Then you know Dynas is not a hospitable world. Like so many across the galaxy, humans are an ill fit." Felix's body moved on its own, its parts wriggling about, as he spoke. Disgusting and fascinating in equal measure. "What I am is a failed attempt to fix our physical nature."

"Join the swamp to colonize the swamp?" Aurora said. "Can't we leave these worlds to the species that want them?"

"For the answer to that you'll need to ask the ones who made me."

Aurora, and Sever in general, were definitely not

police. Their job description did not include catching law breakers unless hired specifically to do so. While whomever had engaged in the extreme genetic playing required to create something like Felix had broken all manner of galactic laws and norms, it was, to be frank, not Aurora's problem.

"I'll settle for a way out, and my squad's safety," Aurora said. "Unless I'm reading this wrong, you have some control over this base?"

Felix spoke like a leader. A person who'd fallen into power without necessarily looking for it, and while they weren't comfortable wearing this particular cloak, they would bear it nonetheless.

"I do, and I do not," Felix said. "I am a rogue that has gone ignored long enough to find new problems to solve, ones that you could help me with."

"We're already on a job, sorry."

"Perhaps I could change your mind? You haven't heard my offer."

"Surprise me, then."

Whatever his appearance, and Felix looked like he could offer next to nothing, the galaxy had shown Aurora time and again that rejecting potentials out of hand led to missed opportunities. If Felix had something that could command more value to Sever than pursuing their job, Aurora had the leeway to take it.

The projectors in the room's corners flashed and Felix's image disappeared, instead turning into four identical, tall and wire-thin creatures in the room's corners. Each one looked like a scrawnier, weaker version of Felix, though their faces showed an impressive diversity in skin-tone, age, and sex. Whomever made these things didn't care to discriminate. Otherwise, they were even uglier than Felix, their growths blackened and dropping slime that faded and disappeared as the things took shaking steps towards Aurora.

As disgusting as they looked, as their misshapen shamble revealed their muscles in evident decay, the silence of their approach, the total lack of sound or warning beep from her visor messed with Aurora more. She had nothing to fear from the things coming near her, they were only projections, yet they seemed so, so real.

Aurora fired the rifle before she really realized what she was doing. The bright laser burned through the closest projection, splitting it in half and sending its charred bits to the ground, where they fizzled in the projection's light. Wait. That shouldn't have happened, unless these projectors could handle . . .

The slime gripped Aurora's right shoulder from behind, its weight plenty real. Aurora didn't turn, but jabbed her elbow back, knocking the smaller creature away from her. Then Aurora burst forward, darting towards the remaining creature in front of her, firing two torching bolts that downed the monster. She could worry about how Felix managed to turn his projections into real, living things later. A whirl around brought Aurora face to face with the last two creatures, both walking towards her with vine arms stretched out, like the zombies in so many movies.

And like those zombies, they too went down in fast fire.

As the last bits of their gooey bodies settled on the ground, Felix reappeared in the room's center, a sad frown on his face, "Those were far from the best of us. The early versions did not turn out so well, but I believe they still understood."

Aurora shot Felix. The bolt, though, sizzled through the moss-thing's body without affecting anything and blasted into the computer setup in the far corner, sending sparks cascading, starting a small fire, and popping the room's lights back on. The illumination turned Felix into a pale, wispy version of himself, who looked directly at Aurora as she confirmed, with a quick sweep of her eyes, that no other nasty surprises waited for her.

"You fared better than your friend," Felix said. "As I said, I have an offer for you."

"And I already have a job."

Aurora snapped off four shots, each bolt striking one of the projectors and sending Felix's image fading out. Not the best use, maybe, of her rifle's charge, but she had more power packs with her.

Felix might have one of Sever's members, he might not, but Aurora knew one thing for sure, as she contemplated the door sealing her in the room, Felix would not be keeping them. Not after trying to kill her.

She already had a job: to find Felix, and burn him to ash.

TWENTY-TWO

The Black City

SKIFFS HELD strong as the cheapest transport on civilized worlds. They offered few amenities, no defense against the elements or more dangerous things, and tended to break down at inopportune moments, plummeting into city streets and forcing their passengers to dive through nearby windows to avoid becoming a meaty splatter.

Sai had experienced his fill of skiffs—that crash on Sirus Nine had been the last time he'd set foot on one of these wrecks—but here he was, coasting through a yellow miasma towards an unknown destination on another one.

Sirus Nine had been a rough mission, a semi-urban planet ravaged by uprisings against corrupt leadership who knew enough to get a DefenseCorp extraction when things took a sharp dip towards the unsustainable.

Sai and Sever had been on the skiffs heading towards the extraction point when the breakdown had occurred. The whole way Sai had been chatting with Gregor about who had the right of it: those corrupt leaders who sold out the planet time and time again, or the populace who'd put all those people into office in the first place. Gregor sided with the people, and Sai couldn't keep up a defense for very long: as a father, it was awfully hard to argue for vipers sucking away their planet's resources for their own interstellar machinations, even if Sai had seen the devastation uprisings like Sirus Nine's could cause.

Then again, the escape had worked. DefenseCorp had extracted all of them and sent the leaders to their shiny new ships, ready to cruise the nebulae for a few centuries before finding some new place to poison.

Wouldn't it be funny if those same leaders wound up here, begging for extraction all over again?

"Hey, you listening?" Eponi's call made it through Sai's reverie. "I'm trying to tell you we're getting close to something big."

"I thought the skiff locked you out?"

Sai turned back towards the skiff's pilot house. He couldn't see Eponi in there, hunched around the monitors. Couldn't see much out here either. Just mist. Everwhere.

"It's flying a dummy route, not trying to kill us." Eponi made a bright noise that said she found something. "It's even bigger. Huge. Like, a city."

"A city in this?"

Sai had seen worse locales—Artek, home to more lava than Sai ever needed to see, required its people to wear heat suits at all times to avoid melting away—but the idea of settling on Dynas and spending every day staring up at this stuff would be close to the worst. He'd need a lot of cash to make it worth it. A *lot* of cash. Like—

The skiff kept moving, but the mist stopped. The green-yellow morass flattened and spread away from Sai as the skiff flowed through a barrier that made Sai's skin tingle. His armor popped up a notification that Sai had crossed an electrified threshold. Hard white light shone down from a suddenly clear sky, crashing into Sai and forcing him to flip to a darkened visor to keep himself from getting blinded.

The real wonder lay below, spreading out behind what looked like a large sea wall. The wall's top glowed a neon yellow, cluing Sai into the barrier's true nature.

Sai wouldn't call himself a nanobot expert, but the micro-machines had spread so far throughout the galaxy by this point that simply paying attention would tell you the possibilities. The little suckers could be manufactured by the trillions for cheap and set with almost any protocol, like stopping any yellow mist-tainted air, from getting through their shield. Humans like Sai and things like the skiff would fall outside the nanobot's scope, and the tiny machines would flow aside and let'em through. The barrier wouldn't be perfect, but get those nanobots dense enough, and you could have a pretty good prevention mechanism.

And one that could be changed to target just about any threat, like an enemy squad.

"You ever hear of this place?" Eponi said, joining up near the front of the skiff.

"Apparently I should have," Sai replied. "It's huge."

"I said that already."

"Thought it needed to be repeated."

The city itself didn't have the splendor shared between the galaxy's flagship planets, even if it seemed to have the size. Few large buildings rose from a landscape covered in squat housing, almost all of them with crop-covered roofs. Self-sustaining efforts then, which, given Dynas's apparent crappiness and the lack of interstellar traffic, would be necessary to keep people alive and well.

Normal traffic, on the other hand, appeared healthy. Other skiffs and small transports fluttered around the skies, and beneath him, Sai could see passenger cars shuttling civilians around. A true city.

"What do you think it's for?" Eponi said as the skiff continued its trek inward. "What would you even do here?"

"No idea." An honest answer. Without the intergalactic trade, there didn't seem to be an obvious idea. Unless Dynas had a large native contingent, or colonists that wanted nothing to do with the rest of the galaxy. "Maybe some sort of anti-establishment sect?"

"With outposts coated in turrets and a bunch of guards?"

"You're asking me to guess, but you know what?" Sai pointed down at the city. "I checked the coordinates. The signal we're hunting came from down there."

"I'm not jumping, if that's what you're thinking."

Sai peered over the edge and let his visor bounce the distance from the skiff to the surface. About half a kilometer. Too far in armor, and Eponi didn't even have that. This wouldn't turn into an airborne assault, and given the number of guards back at that outpost, Sai didn't relish the idea of a two-person attack on the city.

"Think it'd be better if we took this skiff back and picked up the others," Sai replied. "Now that we know where we're going . . ."

"If you have any ideas on how to get this skiff to listen, you're free to try."

Sai grimaced, but Eponi had a point. He wasn't a hacker, but Sai might be able to bypass the skiff's computers and make the craft a dumb, flying brick. Not exactly the smartest maneuver, but if the only other option meant riding this skiff to wherever it wanted them to go . . . Sai had to give it a shot.

"Let me know if I need to get my head outta the

wires," Sai said as he clomped back towards the pilot house.

"Oh, I'll scream real loud."

Inside, Sai looked at the triple monitors showing the skiff's vitals and its intended route. Beneath the screens sat the metal casing that ought to house the real goods. Easy-access screws proved Dynas at least adopted some galactic standards—making critical systems difficult to get at made crashes more likely, and newer setups like this made Sai's job far easier. Some quick work with the multitool popped off the cover plate and revealed a cable bird's nest inside. Various colors coated the wires themselves, giving Sai a rainbow's worth to work with.

Sai had to cut the cable feed from the pilot's computer to the skiff's central system. Slice that, and the skiff would, hopefully, fall into panic mode. Would let Sai or Eponi take the manual controls and use the flight stick to wheel the skiff back towards Sever and the smaller base. Cut the wrong cable, and Sai could leave them powerless, or send the skiff into a nosedive.

No pressure.

He swapped the multitool to its microlaser, turned on his helmet light, and peered in close. No clear indicators, but Sai could get some ideas from the wire's thickness, the amount of data they'd be sending along. A likely candidate loomed in the middle, a deep purple color. He held up the multitool.

"You ready to run back here if this works?" Sai asked, having to shout and hope Eponi could hear.

"I'm right next to you." Eponi leaned down, put her hand on Sai's shoulder. "You really lose yourself in this stuff."

"If I don't, I'm dead," Sai replied. "Get ready."

He fired the laser, cut the wire, which sent sparks flying,

which did not send the skiff into a dive. Sai exhaled slow. Waited. No alarms, no beeps.

"Can you take control?" Sai asked.

"It's not moving."

The skiff, though, had other ideas. Before Sai could back out from the wires and try to learn what he'd actually cut, the skiff swung sharply right, banging Sai's helmet against the maintenance alcove. Eponi yelped, and Sai felt a drag around his waist as she grabbed his armor. The skiff stabilized, swinging back level, and Sai exited to try and get some idea of what he'd done. The monitors, though, were blank. Sheer black, and yet the skiff had changed direction with no switch to manual control.

"What's happening?" Sai asked, not so much as a question to Eponi, but one to himself.

"What'd you cut?"

"The monitors," Sai pointed to the black screens. "Without computer guidance, the skiff should give us manual control."

"Unless it's slaved."

"What?"

Eponi left the pilot house, went back to the deck and Sai followed her there. They were still over the city, but they'd changed direction, heading towards the outer edge and a giant structure that sat there, black spear towers lancing up into the sky. By far the biggest building Sai had seen here, and the only one with a design that spoke of something other than ugly efficiency, the towers iced his mood. The distress call hadn't come from there, but Sai had no doubt whatever waited for them would be worse.

"Slaved means that when it gets hurt," Eponi said, "the skiff goes home."

TWENTY-THREE

A Bright Idea

———————————

As BEDS WENT, a metal floor and armor were crap. Gregor had slept on rock before—working on a comet mandated that experience—and you could lock the armor into a standing position to give you a chance at forty winks while waiting for a mission to start, but actually lying down? His back played Gregor an achy symphony for his choices, even as his visor told Gregor he'd been out for only a few minutes.

Felix's creatures gooped over him, black and purple twisted shadows in the room's scarlet light. Gregor pulled his senses together one by one, shaking off the knockout's after-effects and bringing him back in tune with consciousness. With decisions that needed to be made.

Gregor's armor splayed one warning after another over the visor, indicating various components were, to various degrees, in danger of falling off or disintegrating under the continuous assault from the slime creatures. An assault, Gregor realized, consisting of slow digestion and molecular recombination. Not exactly a phrase that came easily to mind, but that's what the visor told him.

"Simplify," Gregor whispered, an unnatural act for him, but necessary given the circumstances.

The visor caught the command and shifted the display to show Gregor's armor in an overlay, with orange areas representing the spots Felix's swarm had decided to attack. A timeline dropped beneath the armor, and two arrows indicated the visor's attempt to project into the future. Time shifted and the orange grew, devouring Gregor's armor and turning it into more orange until nothing remained.

Clear enough.

"Hammer?" Gregor tried, and the helmet traced the connection between the armor and his chosen weapon.

On the floor, not far from Gregor's own feet, the hammer sent back its own status report: healthy. Waiting to be picked up. To destroy.

Gregor could facilitate.

As the monsters loomed over him, dripping the dissolving sludge onto Gregor's face, chest, and everywhere else, the Sever squad enforcer simultaneously flexed his arms and legs, a combined muscle movement designed to trigger a particular response: lightning shocks erupted from tiny nodes across the armor, drawing from power that could otherwise be used for Gregor's rifle. Enough energy to start small fires, to melt through skin. The blue-white arcs chained up the goop and enveloped the creatures in fiery pockets.

Gregor took the opening and sat up, mind reeling from the shift for a hot second before adrenaline overcame the nausea and let Gregor climb to his feet. Felix, the projectors causing him to shimmer, faced him. The half-human, half-fungus looked bemused at Gregor's attempt to free himself, and while Gregor wished he could take his gauntlets and crush Felix between his armored palms, sanity dictated he walk right through the image and pick up his hammer.

"It will only end the same way as before," Felix said as Gregor hefted the weapon. "There are too many of us. So many failed experiments looking for new possibilities."

"Shut it." Gregor looked at the ceiling, flipped his visor to infrared as the slime creatures approached him.

While picking up the hammer, Gregor noticed the creatures were all over the room. Whether Felix had opened the door and let more of the things in, or if they had other means of accessing the space, their numbers had grown so that the room appeared a writhing, black mass. Gross, and something Gregor would have enjoyed crushing, except he'd already seen what fighting these things would mean: they'd fall from above, strike from below, and splatter every part of him with offal until Gregor couldn't move, couldn't breathe. Delivering glorious smashes with the hammer wasn't worth that risk.

So as the monsters reached their fungal tendrils towards his legs, as they caressed his back and dripped onto his head, Gregor looked to the ceiling and saw, behind the creature's light purple-orange insides, the thick red-white bar showing the base's heat exhaust. One of several, likely, needed to keep the base at an optimal temperature despite all the equipment burning away down here, creating these things, keeping the power running for the guards above. The asteroid Gregor had grown up on had plenty of these, just to keep things inside the rock from getting too hot.

"What are you looking at?" Felix asked.

Gregor didn't say anything, just pulled his arm back and launched the hammer straight towards the ceiling.

Black slime wrapped around his neck, his knees, his arms as they completed the swing. The silent monsters coming closer. For the moment.

The hammer broke through the sludge and slammed into the ceiling, delivering its packed energy charge in a breaking burst that rippled along the tiles, splitting them apart and raining goop down among the creatures. Goop followed by a wave of heat, released and flaring into bright fire as it touched the creature's soft, very flammable fungus bodies. What had been a red-stained, dark room became an inferno.

Gregor knelt within it, letting his armor close its heat shields to keep him protected, a stone within the firestorm.

The very first posting from DefenseCorp had stuck Gregor on a sun-baked rock, aptly nicknamed Roast, in a far-flung system where he'd been tasked with watching over a mining city whose populace, under the heavy thumb of its ruling, and providing, company existed to plumb the planet's depths and pick out rare jewels created by the combination of surface heat and subsurface pressure.

Gregor thought Roast's surface resembled glass more than sand, and they'd all worn heat-dispersing suits to survive. Part of keeping the city, domed with black solar panels to provide energy and, through screens, simulate the passing of a more normal day, livable involved sending all that heat out through massive vents. The openings cycled through the dome, little slits appearing in the perfect, simu-lated sky.

Massive fans served to push cold air down, hot air up towards those vents, and Gregor would watch the rooftop blades whirl from his outpost in the city's center, their waved streams showing the heat's steady climb out. They also served as a beacon for anyone looking to send a message to the city, or to leave it in fiery despair. Jump into one of those streams and, suit or no, you'd be molten in moments. Gregor's contract said to protect the city. It did not say to keep its people from hurting themselves.

So they would watch, during those simulated nights, for the occasional orange burst showing one more miner giving in.

Gregor had taken the first opportunity to leave that contract behind, but he'd never forget those flares. For what it was worth, Gregor could thank them now for the idea that'd saved his own life.

"Another surprise," Felix said as the flames died away, the base compensating for the broken vent and redirecting its energies elsewhere. "I continue to underestimate you and your friend."

"My friend?" Gregor said, his helmet's filter letting in the air and its charred smell.

The slime creatures existed now only as ashen pools across the room. Black bits hung from the ceiling, seared into place. Others, their fungal arms looking like candles, folded in on themselves as their insides roasted away. An ugly sight turned even worse.

But Gregor lived.

"Yes. She reacted much as you did when I confronted her." Felix turned slow around the room, taking in the whole display. "She didn't want to help me, but thankfully, she did. As did you."

"Helped?" Gregor picked up his hammer, kept his eyes moving.

What other tricks did this thing have?

"Oh yes. Cleared my way, so to speak." Felix gestured towards the broad door, and at his motion, the soot-stained thing rattled up and open. "I think you are about done here. Please, take the tram and leave."

"I don't take orders from you."

"Then consider it a suggestion." Felix shrugged. "Leave and live, stay and die. It's all the same to me."

TWENTY-FOUR

Split Decision

LOSING control of her vehicle numbered way up on the list of things that made Eponi freak out. The ideal piloting experience, with her hands on the controls, had Eponi feeling like the vehicle existed with her, another limb, or, really, another part of her mind. Think one thing and the vehicle would do that thing almost at the same instant. Her short racing career had been built on that fact, had thrived by the way she could carve up the twisting ridge lines of icy worlds and rocky ones alike, how she could swoop beneath or loop through her opponent's wreckage as they failed to do the same.

And then she'd gone and done that stupid thing.

No. Not falling down that memory hole again, though the parallels were inescapable as Eponi tried to yank the skiff's flight stick, tried to turn it anywhere but where it faced now: that dark tower. Eponi didn't quite know what to call it, but she knew a slaved circuit would be taking them someplace with plenty more guards. Plenty more people interested in why a skiff that'd left with a crew returned with two enemies instead.

"Any ideas?" Sai asked, staring at her. "You still have no control?"

"I'm trying to get this to work because it makes me feel better," Eponi replied. "The skiff's never going to give this back to me. Not unless we burrowed into the heart of this thing and tore out the circuit itself."

"Is that possible?"

"Sure, let's break apart the thing we're flying in, *while we're flying.*"

"Right," Sai said. "Good point."

The demolitionist decided his opinions provided little value to Eponi's state of mind and left, heading out to the deck. Maybe he wanted to prep some assault plan. Go in with his sword and cut down everyone. That'd be a fun play. DefenseCorp didn't exactly forbid Sever from racking up collateral damage on its missions, but it kept a pretty clear profit and loss statement for every debrief, and Sai taking down a tower filled with innocents would probably swing this particular column into the red.

As extra costs were taken out of Sever's pay, that seemed a poor call, unless Sever could prove the tower, the city, and everyone living here played a part in some nefarious conspiracy to kill them. Which, if that was true, Eponi might as well give up now because Sever only had five members and not nearly enough artillery to take on a planet.

The thought sparked an idea: if all-out fighting, or any fighting at all, would be a bad call for the two Severs on the skiff, then the alternative meant stealth. Given the tower's approach and the skiff's dwindling altitude—it looked like, Eponi saw from peaking out the pilot's house entry—that they were headed towards some mid-level docking bay. Sai could probably jump out with his armor. While Sai's streaking missile would be visible to anyone who cared to look, it might tear some eyes away from Eponi, allowing her to . . . do what, exactly? Claim she'd been forced on to the skiff by the enemy?

Even if that plan didn't turn Sai outright into meat pudding upon impact, Eponi didn't want to rely on her deception skills to get her inside whatever mysterious group controlled this place. She knew too little to pass off as anything under cursory interrogation. The only way to sneak out of this would be with a hefty distraction, something that could get her out of the grip of whomever they were coasting in to meet with minimal capture, maximum chaos.

"Skiff, I know our time was brief, but I think I'm going to have to blow you up," Eponi said to the dead monitors. There was no response. "Sai! Get back in here!"

With heavy clomps barely covered by the softening whine from the skiff's jets, no longer tasked with keeping the craft high in the sky, Sai returned, looking as confused as ever in his armor.

"You get an idea?"

"I did," Eponi said, pointing at the monitors. "What kind of arsenal are you packing?"

"I have three mines left. A couple bigger explosives." Sai glanced at the monitors. "I thought you were against destroying the ship we're flying on?"

"Hear me out," Eponi said. "Put one of your big bangers towards the front. The very front. We detonate when the skiff goes in, take cover in the pilot house. It goes up, everyone freaks out, and then we make a break for it."

"You don't have any armor."

Eponi looked down at herself, back up at Sai. "When was the last time you looked at me?"

"Now?"

"What do you see?"

"Uh, a person?"

"A tiny person. You wrap me up like a ball, and we've got this." Eponi had squeezed into smaller cockpits, for sure. "Skiff goes boom, we break out."

Sai clamped his armored hands over the top of his head, like some mechanized ballerina dancer. A move Sai did from time to time whenever the man seriously contemplated an idea. At least Eponi's suggestion merited that.

"You're going to die," Sai concluded.

"That's up to you. But we're out of time, and if you don't get that bomb set, we're both gonna die for sure. Maybe go a little light on the explosives?"

Sai turned back towards the skiffs deck, looked out the pilot house for a moment, then clomped out. "Not my fault if this doesn't go your way."

"If it doesn't," Eponi called after him. "I won't be alive to care."

She hated being shot at. Hated being on the front lines. Yet, here, getting ready to self-destruct their skiff as the tower's welcoming green lights began to play over them, Eponi felt giddy. Like she was back in one of her races, with every second on the dividing edge between life and instant, explosive death. Getting shot was terrifying, succeeding in a daring move like this? Well, that was no different than juking out Wezzak Cav to take first place in the Erunian Classic.

To juke, though, Eponi needed to see, so she left the pilot's house as the skiff began to enter the vast docking bay. Up close, the tower revealed itself to be less the product of sinister medieval fantasies and more a techno-construct like most of the buildings it overlooked; the dark color came from solar panels sucking energy from the white starlight crashing down from above. Useless without the nanobots clearing the mist, but with those, Eponi felt the whole place probably did pretty well. Not that she knew anything about solar energy, but given how many lights popped from small alcoves to focus on them, including more than a few tracking turrets, the tower had power to burn.

Straight glass windows striped the tower, breaking between solar panels, and Eponi could see shapes moving on the other side. Not great that she and Sai, who had crouched down at the skiff's bow to plant the bomb, had little cover. She crept back, slid against the pilot house's inside wall and peered out. Slight protection from wandering eyes, but better than nothing. The tower seemed populated, though Eponi had no idea what the hour was relative to Dynas's day and night schedule, what work hours were on the planet, or even whether the people she saw were workers or something more. Or less. All dossier material that DefenseCorp would have provided if, well, they'd known this place existed.

"You almost ready?" Eponi called. "Because we're almost out of time!"

"It'll be set," Sai shouted back. "Get ready!"

The docking bay swallowed them like a neon green mouth, the lights lining the bay's edges serving as guides to pilots who could actually control their skiffs. Eponi watched them slide overhead—their skiff now traveled at a sedate walking pace for the landing—and saw the bay's ceiling, coated with tubes, robotic hooks and wheels, cranes and all manner of maintenance tools Eponi would have expected to find in the bay a broken skiff would choose. If anything, this would break in their favor; maybe whomever ran this place wouldn't be sending their defenses to greet a busted craft.

Sai pushed into her, dashing his bulk back and pressing them into the pilot's house, "They've got a squad down there, at least," Sai said. "Pretty sure they saw me too."

"Blowing our cover before we even start?"

"I haven't blown anything yet." Sai sat on the floor, his legs bending up at the knees like he was just taking a quick break. In the armor, it looked ridiculous. "Squeeze in here and I'll do what I can. We only have a few seconds."

The skiff slowed even further, and Eponi felt the skiff's landing jets take over as she slid against Sai's chest. She pulled her legs in, cradled her pistol tight in her arms and tucked her chin against her chest. Sai wrapped his arms around her, pulled his legs in around hers as best he could, and rested his head forward on top of hers. Not perfect cover, but close. The best they could hope for.

"Don't let me die here," Eponi said, soft.

"Not planning on it."

"Nobody ever does."

There wasn't a clue. No moment to prepare. In one second the skiff existed, whole and slightly damaged, making a landing in front of a suspicious but not overly excited inspection squad. In the next, concussive bangs separated the skiff's front third from the rest of it, splitting the bow into a thousand speeding metal spears that sprayed across the bay, piercing walls, people, and anything else with a propulsive lethality. Eponi couldn't see any of this, she couldn't hear any of it either as the blast knocked her hearing into a ringing echo. Eponi did feel the skiff's aft whirl around, its jets attempting to compensate for the sudden loss of mass and the cataclysmic damage to the skiff's body. Rather than launch back out of the docking bay—a momentary fear—the skiff wheeled about before settling into a sliding crash against one of the bay's long side walls, barreling through equipment and the wall itself.

Somewhere during that rending crash, the entire pilot

house tore off and away in a sparking shower, the ripping metal sound shearing through Eponi's blasted hearing. Sai kept himself locked around her, kept the raining shrapnel from cutting through, from killing her. Eponi forgave Sai, in that instant, for every mistake he'd ever made. For his obsession with that sword. For anything and everything.

She just wanted to live.

TWENTY-FIVE

Work Life Balance

HE CAME from a paper pusher family. The phrase stuck around—Rovo's father employed it liberally, with pride— despite actual paper having little use whatsoever in the modern world. The family anthem stood on dependable, unstressed hours. Predictable income and a work-life balance so even that contented existence seemed a given. Rovo, following this template prescribed by his ancestors, would have himself a family, time for hobbies, and a quiet, virtuous life spent shuttling data from one corner of the galaxy to another.

"You might think it boring," his father had told him after trouncing a seventeen year-old Rovo in another game of 4D-chess. "But there's something to be said for steadiness. I'm here, aren't I? How many other families can say that?"

Rovo couldn't. Not anymore. He'd thrown off familiarity's yoke for excitement. His parents had objected, but DefenseCorp didn't care. They wanted bodies on the front lines, collecting higher rates on dangerous planets. Translations and other desk work could be handled, if not by machines, then by other, fresher recruits from copious sentient species with no desire to wield rifles. Rovo had taken the leap, and hadn't seen his family since. Might never see them again if he couldn't get out of this office, off of this planet.

The monitors still showed the words, called Rovo 'food', though for what, Rovo didn't know. Presumably for the color that had devoured all the rest in that strange game, but no red blobs presented themselves. Instead, Rovo watched the door and considered his options. Charge out and take a gamble that other Sever members had drawn the guards away? Stay here and stay hidden, and hope that the crisis would somehow resolve itself? Try again with the computers—maybe the words came from a program and, knowing the rules of the game, Rovo could win this time.

No. He'd joined Sever to be a part of the action, not to run from it.

Still in his bulky, laser-burned armor, Rovo rose to his feet and went towards the office door. Outside the small windows scarlet lights blazed in the hallways. Alarms continued to blare, giving truth to the continued emergency or to the possibility that nobody remained to shut the awful noise off. Whatever; as inconveniences went, Rovo could deal with a little sound.

He poked his finger at the switch and the door obeyed, swishing open and giving Rovo access to the outside. With his assault rifle in his hands, Rovo dipped a look to the right, back towards the power plant, and found himself facing the dangerous end of another weapon. A guard stood there, staring at him.

"Central told us we had a problem over here," the guard said, his voice young, black skin suit fresh and clean. "Guess they were right."

"You're going to back into that office real slow," another voice spoke, behind Rovo. This one a woman, older. Equal opportunity enemies. "Set that rifle down right here, or we'll burn you. At this range, wouldn't think that armor of yours would work real well."

Rovo wasn't so sure about that. DefenseCorp tended to outfit its premier units with the best possible gear—training up skilled soldiers took more money than buying specialized equipment—and part of him wanted to ignore the orders, blaze the guards down and take his chances. But then, discretion and valor and all that. Better to get both guards in that little office than leave one ready to burn him in the back.

"I'm heading back in," Rovo said, laying the rifle at his metal-clad feet and retreating back inside the office. "How'd you two sneak up on me? I didn't see you through the windows."

The two guards, implacable in their full black suits, said nothing as they followed Rovo into the office, shutting the door behind them. Neither picked up Rovo's rifle; a shame, as the weapon was tied to Rovo's suit signature. Anyone else trying to use it would find the thing nothing more than an expensive club. Instead, they kept their smaller, one-handed pistols aimed right for Rovo's face.

"You were heads-down staring at the screens," the first guard said. "You've got equipment that says you're bankrolled. By who?"

"Not your problem." Rovo dredged up the bravado from the movies he'd seen. Clung to it and waited for an opportunity. "I want to know—"

"You don't get to ask the questions." The same guard stuck his spitter closer to Rovo's face, as if the barrel's black nozzle would make Rovo talk. Which, it might. Lasers were scary things. "Who sent you, and how many of you are there?"

"Only one of me, baby," Rovo replied.

"About to be zero," the second guard said.

A rumbling blast punctuated her words, the base trembling and throwing both guards off their aim. Rovo, his heavier feet keeping their balance, dove forward, stretching out his arms in a wide tackle. Rovo hit both guards and carried them to the floor as the rumbling died away, new sounds added to the alarms. When they hit the ground, Rovo had no strategy. No technique. He just pounded with his elbows, with his fists and knees against the struggling guards. Both seemed to be gasping for air after the initial tackle, and that made their escape efforts weak, half-hearted. Rovo couldn't tell how effective his hits were through the suits, but eventually the guards stopped moving. Rovo threw another pair of punches to confirm the two were down, then he stole away their pistols and snapped them.

The movies said a moment would come, and it had. Rovo laughed, the giddy sort that comes with an unexpected victory. His former co-workers had treated Rovo's decision to jump off to DefenseCorp's active arm with the skepticism reserved for the truly insane. His parents had been the same, telling Rovo he wasn't cut out for this sort of thing, that none of them were. Excitement should be reserved for the copious virtual realms, not lived in real life. Now he stood victorious. A Sever.

"Stability can suck it," Rovo muttered.

In the hall, Rovo picked up his abandoned rifle and faced his options. The office monitors had swapped screens with the explosion to a read out of the base's various calamities, starting with Sever's intrusion to the most recent event, the rupture of a major heat exhaust vent.

The computer didn't say what had caused the damage, but Rovo felt he could chalk it up to something his teammates had done.

Walking disasters, all of them. The best kind.

Two options. Back towards the power plant, where Sai had blown his barricade, or deeper into the base. More office doors greeted that option, with a sharp bend in the hallway cutting off further guesses. No signage either. Still, the guards likely came with the squad running in through the broken front door, which led to the power plant. Which meant Rovo ought to go the other way.

As Aurora put it often enough in their meetings: seek the objective, not a fight.

Around the hallway's bend, the path splintered into more right angled cast-offs. Warning signs appeared. Windowless doors with badge-scanning sensors. Shock-white spray labeled the rooms with nonsensical letter and number combinations. Code, like the transmissions Rovo had sought, failed to crack. Now he had a hallway trio to choose from, each lit in blaze red and leading off somewhere.

Except something moved in the central hall. Down there, at the light's very edge. Roughly human-shaped, but the outline didn't match the armor worn by the other guards. Shorter and bulkier too. The shape seemed to stare at him, and Rovo raised his rifle.

"Stay still!" Rovo shouted over the alarms. "Or I'll shoot!"

The form didn't reply. Rovo flipped his visor to infrared and saw green, orange. The thing was alive, then. Not some robot.

Cool blue-black pooled around the blob; no other living things hiding around the corner, either. The thing was alone. Rovo could leave it, break down one of the other hallways and see what he found, but he didn't relish turning his back on whatever this was. And he did like getting some information. This thing might know where the rest of Sever had gone, or at least this place's purpose.

Rovo went slow. Walking with his assault rifle ready, vision back to normal so he could see the thing's body straight ahead. Could see when what Rovo thought were clothes turned out to be strange lumps instead, could see a pair of bright blue eyes shaded not by hair but, instead, by something altogether more solid. Thick. What was this thing? Rovo had the suit dissect the air, splash an analysis over the visor as he went. No abnormalities—the base recycled its air, and aside from usual particulates from living people, nothing seemed off. Rovo tried to think of other potential traps, but he couldn't see a weapon anywhere. So what did this thing, who refused to say a word, actually want?

Halfway down the center branch, bracketed between a pair of steel doors bearing what looked like greenish-black mold spreading around the edges, Rovo stopped when the alarms fell silent. Having lived with their constant yowling for what was minutes but felt like years, the sudden silence echoed. The creature didn't seem to care except to tilt its head to the side, as if asking Rovo what he thought about this turn of events.

The lights went dark.

Rovo's helmet ran faster than his reflexes and swapped him to night-vision, which sucked in every possible photon to create a blurry green picture, in time to catch the creature shambling away around another bend.

"Stop!" Rovo shouted, but he received no response.

Who had extinguished the alarms, the lights? Rovo keyed into his transmitter and listened to the guards' encrypted chatter. Excited, definitely, but impossible to tell if this was their move or someone else's. Aurora or Gregor, maybe? Sai and Eponi knew their way around tech. Could be they torched everything to hide somewhere.

"Anyone read me?" Rovo tried another message on the squad's frequency and heard nothing for it. No other chatter either. "Guess not."

Which left following the creature as the only worthwhile option. Rovo quick-stepped after it, though he played by the rules and peeked around the bend, rifle ready, before stepping out of cover. The corner progressed for a short burst before dead-ending into another door, this one bearing a wide range of hazardous signs in addition to a quadruple zero label. A small hole to the door's right revealed a sparking wire, which flared bright to Rovo, and pieces of what must have been the broken scanner scattered on the floor.

No creature, though.

Rovo crept towards the door, noting the molding edges here too. The base needed a good scrubbing, seemed like. Better to hold to that idea than consider the less lovely options why high-grade metal like this would be corroding. Better to stay focused and not go wandering down more dangerous paths.

"Open sesame," Rovo said, standing in front of the door.

It didn't budge.

But when he put his hand against it, reaching for the slightly indented, darker section labeling the door's switch, the barrier slid aside. Even with the helmet on, the air filter going, Rovo felt the rush as captive atmosphere pressed free around him. Rovo froze for a second, panicking, before stopping himself. This sort of pressure seal tended to mean an airlock, which, for most of Rovo's life, meant he'd be stepping into outer space if he went much farther.

But he wasn't in space, no matter how pitch dark the broad room in front of him was. He'd landed on Dynas. No vacuum here.

He could see a ladder. In front of him and hanging on to a narrow, railed platform, illuminated by a pair of emergency dots embedded into the floor, powering their red through the thin, fleshy web covering it. The green-black tendrils covered the ladder, and grew around the railing too. Spreading across the tiled steel floor in blotches. Rovo stepped over the threshold into the room, went forward and peered over the railing. Too little light down there to see.

Rovo could fix that.

He tapped the top of his helmet, flaring on his light, and looked. Ice took hold at what Rovo saw, and he wanted, really wanted to hold the trigger on his rifle and burn every ounce of the room to ash. But he wouldn't have the energy. A dozen assault rifles wouldn't have the power to burn through all that pulsing, growing awfulness. Black and green, blue and purple, the giant space—Rovo figured it was larger than the power plant—bore all the hallmarks of experiments gone wrong. Shattered glass tubes hung from the ceiling, their bottom halves hidden beneath the shifting pool.

And what a pool. Like a rotten soup still boiling, the rippling dark popped and bubbled, waved and writhed. Whether the movement came from the stuff itself or something beneath it, Rovo didn't know. Didn't want to know.

Sever had come here to save someone needing rescue, not deal with horrors like this. Time to go back. Find Aurora and get the hell away from here.

Rovo turned back to the door. Standing in front of it, between him and the exit from this nightmare chamber, was the creature in all its gross glory.

"I'm so glad you came," it said, and pushed.

Rovo's armor compensated for the shove, tried to lock his feet down, but Rovo stood on the mold, and the mold pushed back. Rovo slipped, tried to grab the railing as the creature pushed him again.

He fell.

TWENTY-SIX

Monster Hunting

GROWING up on a space ship meant Aurora spent time dealing with locked doors. Giving children free rein in a structure covered in buttons that could, depending on the circumstance, vent oxygen, blow emergency shuttles into space, or adjust greenhouse temps was universally acknowledged to be a terrible idea.

Yet, as larger and larger ships increasingly served as endless homes for the people living on them as they traversed the galaxy from one system to another, childcare methods had to be developed. For Aurora and the dozen other kids on the *Skysurf*, that meant spending most days sealed off in a domed room, staring at nebulae above and trying to crack their way to freedom below.

They'd never managed it then, toys proving to be poor tools for breaking modern locks.

Now, though, Aurora had a pair of small strike busters, little mines that'd glue onto a point and blow it open. This door had a bit more size than the mines were designed for, and no obvious weak point to target, but after reviewing the monitor's smoldering ruin, Aurora didn't see another way out. She'd felt an explosion two minutes ago, but when the base didn't collapse on her, Aurora figured she'd still need to blow her own exit.

She kept trying Sever's squad channel too, encountering only static. When they made it back to DefenseCorp, Aurora would force their stingy buyers to get them some communicators capable of penetrating a floor's worth of metal. Or at least try, because this mess was maddening. How could Aurora command her force if she couldn't talk to them?

Well, they'd hear the bang from these mines, anyway.

Aurora pulled the first one off. A small disk with four diamond drills on its back, the strike buster could use its tiny battery to gouge a hold where it'd wait for Aurora's signal to blow its charge. She inspected the broad metal door, deciding the thicker walls would be harder to breach. Dead center would present the weakest point. Aurora aimed the strike buster, pressed it against the door and placed her thumb over the surface switch that'd engage the battery.

The door opened fast, shrieking as it rubbed against the diamond teeth, until Aurora jerked the mine away, drawing her pistol with her left hand and aiming it right at Gregor's face.

"Hey," Gregor said, hammer gripped by his side and, apart from the charred black slime coating his armor, looking all right. Beyond him, the hallway still lit scarlet, though the alarms seemed to have stopped. "You okay, commander?"

"It's been a minute."

Aurora moved beyond the door, lest it gather any grand ideas about shutting again, and, in the hallway, she and Gregor debriefed each other about their Felix encounters. Sounded like Gregor took the worst of it—

Aurora hadn't dealt with ceiling-flavored creatures—and the hammer-man wasn't sure how much damage he'd caused to the base, whether it could cope with the destroyed heat vent. Aurora would bet a facility as technical as this one had enough redundancy to keep it from exploding so easily, but a quick departure wouldn't be a bad idea.

But they needed to find the other three before they left. And destroy Felix. In any order.

"The tram's working now," Felix's voice ended their conference. With no projectors in the hallway, the creature couldn't send them his image, but could speak through the scattered intercoms. "I've released the locks. You can leave."

Aurora tried to figure where to look and settled for the tram, "Not leaving till we get the rest of our team. Help us with that, and we might let you live."

She wouldn't, but it generally hurt negotiations to declare one side's impending, certain death.

"Your friends have already left," Felix said. "You are falling behind."

"They would never," Gregor replied. "We are a team."

"Then your team is broken," Felix said. "They flew away on a skiff not long ago, heading towards the city."

Another note to follow-up on, but Aurora didn't want to play investigator in this damn hallway. Instead, she pointed towards the lift with her pistol, "Anyone waiting on the other side of those doors?"

"At the moment, no. In another, who can say?"

Aurora went back, traced Sever's arrival at the base. Eponi had gone on her own to break them in, lost her armor. Aurora and Gregor had split from Rovo and Sai, with the latter two going after Eponi. If the three escaped on the skiff—with their inability to communicate, it wasn't impossible—then Aurora and Gregor might as well hop the tram and say goodbye to this mess.

"How many went on the skiff?" Aurora asked.

"Three," Felix answered, slow and even. Like the very ooze growing all over his body.

That meant they'd found each other. The rest of Sever had left, and Aurora and Gregor ought to follow. Except, if she guessed wrong, if Felix lied . . .

"Show us," Aurora said, and Gregor gave her a confused look, eyes showing through his helmet visor. "If I'm going to trust you, then I need proof. There are cameras everywhere in this base."

Felix didn't answer immediately. A pause long enough that Aurora had already turned to the lift before the slimy voice started again.

"I will, but you must come to me first."

"That's not a problem." Aurora nodded to Gregor, who punched the lift's call panel. "We'll be up soon."

Felix didn't answer. Aurora didn't know where the monster was inside the base, but Felix's creepy attitude and attempts to manipulate and oh, kill her and her team meant she'd be tearing every part of the structure to pieces until she found that slight-smiling face and ripped the fungus off of it.

You didn't threaten Sever and survive.

"He tried to kill me," Gregor said when they both entered the lift. "He failed."

"We won't."

Playing Sever's game meant taking every action with grim intensity. Gregor and Aurora split the lift's sides, each one taking a wall and angling rifles—Gregor slung his hammer into its back slot—at the doors.

When the metal slats slid open, parting from the middle with rapid grace, and revealed a half-dozen guards planning some strategy, the two Severs stitched out so much laser fire that the wall facing the lift started to melt from the heat. The guards didn't get a move in, didn't get to dodge or draw or decide which of those made the better move. The lift doors opened, and ash followed.

"Nobody waiting beyond the lift?" Aurora said as she and Gregor moved out over their victims. "Another lie to answer for."

Felix wouldn't be back towards the base's entrance, which meant going down the other hallway. Red lights still blazed up here too, couching the smoking bodies in crimson shadow. Gregor led, now exchanging his rifles for the hammer while Aurora played support. She kept the transmitter wide open, but only heard static.

The power plant came as a bit of a shock, but confirmed the base's function as something far more than a simple outpost. You didn't run a bunch of micro reactors because you needed to heat up the food at night. A guard pair walked in on Gregor and Aurora from the right hallway, apparently not expecting company despite the warning lights. Aurora snapped a couple bolts, but these guards proved to be faster than the other bunch, diving behind the first reactor as Aurora's fire stitched black holes in the wall behind them.

Gregor went down the power plant's middle, hammer ready, while Aurora went forward towards the hallway the guards had left. Trap them, destroy them. A simple two-step operation. When Aurora rounded the reactor tower, the guards weren't visible. A bang rang through the room, and then there they were, running and firing their pistols behind them towards where Aurora would expect Gregor to be.

"Hi," Aurora said as the guards remembered they were facing two foes, not one. She squeezed the trigger at their faces, their hands flying up in a useless attempt to shield themselves. "Bye."

Gregor came up, walking and swinging the hammer like it was a toy instead of a wrecking machine. Aurora gestured at the downed guards.

"Making me clean up your leftovers?" Aurora said.

"They were cowards."

The hallway the guards had left turned out to be a wreck. Someone had blown apart a wall and collapsed a ceiling into a blocking rubble pile. Sparks fountained from some cut wire, and water leaked out in a spreading pool that Aurora figured might deliver a lethal shock to anyone dumb enough to touch it. They considered the blockage for a moment, before both tossing looks at Gregor's hammer.

"Possible," Gregor said.

"No," Aurora replied. "Not until we rule out the other way."

If the rest of Sever had indeed left, then every minute spent pounding through the wreckage would be a dangerous one. Gregor and Aurora had been handling these guards with surprise's strong support. New reinforcements wouldn't go down so easy. Best to be avoided.

Down the other path they found unconscious soldiers in an office. No laser burns. Sever didn't get bonus points for murders, so Aurora left them there after making sure they had no working weapons. She turned, went back into the hallway, and stopped.

Gregor stood, hammer ready, staring further down. Felix. Difficult to tell precisely in the red light, but Aurora knew the way she knew a threat. Felt it. A tingle on her neck, her breath tightening. She raised her rifle and fired, but Felix moved too quick. Disappeared around the bend.

"Keep it slow," Aurora said. "He wants us to follow him, or he'd vanish already."

"Playing a dangerous game."

"One he'll lose."

Around the bend, the doors changed. What had been offices now bore broader labels, and the shiny walls darkened with running, moldy black lines. As if the base itself were diseased. Aurora made a quick calculation: any doors looking like they harbored plague, she didn't want to see opened. The sight, though, tickled that part of Aurora always attuned to money-making opportunities. The things she'd already seen here broke all manner of galactic norms, but a dozen or so queasy experiments wouldn't get anyone too riled up. A base full of these things, and one like Felix likely meant more, could signal a different response all together.

DefenseCorp paid big bounties for big contracts, and cleaning up a world like Dynas, covered in bio-engineered monsters, would be a big contract. Aurora might be able to retire from the finders-fee alone.

"Branches," Gregor said as the hallway split into three. "Felix is in the middle."

So he was. Standing there in the red. Looking ugly as ever.

"Shoot him?" Gregor asked. "Or should I charge?"

"Let's go slow," Aurora replied. "I'm getting curious to see how far this goes. We can waste him at the end."

Felix didn't object to the pace. Though, when the two Severs made it halfway to him, the creature darted away again. This time, the lights died too, plunging everything dark.

"Lights up," Aurora said, and immediately both of their helmets sprayed the hallway with bright yellow-white. "If Felix wants it dark, we're not going to give it to him."

Gregor took the lead again, hammer ready, and Aurora walked a couple meters back, giving him plenty of swinging room. She checked their backs constantly, but nothing tried to spring an ambush. They reached a closed door, heavily labeled. No badge scanner.

"Ready?" Gregor asked.

"Ready."

He touched the door and it slid open without protest. Revealed a small platform and a ladder. Gregor took a long step out, peered over the edge. Aurora's light caught the shadow, and she dashed forward—as much as one could in the bulky armor—and slammed Felix's arm down. She followed the strike onto the platform as Felix shrank away to the right, where he'd apparently been hiding beneath a hollowed out console. A trap, then. Aurora aimed her rifle as Gregor flipped to a left-handed swing. She could roast, he could crush.

"How do you want to die?" Aurora asked.

"I don't want to die," Felix replied.

"Not a choice," Gregor answered.

"A bargain!" Felix said. "Information for my life. For your friend's."

"You said our friends were gone," Aurora said, not surprised in the slightest.

"They did not grow me to be honest."

"How about afraid?"

"That, I do know," Felix said, climbing, sponging, his way out of his hollow. "Your friend. He is down there."

With a sickly, fungal arm, Felix pointing down beyond the ladder, to the gurgling, black and green mold mass. Aurora could see, sticking out like a planted flag, Rovo's leg, blue armor shining in her helmet light.

TWENTY-SEVEN

Hard Landing

DEFENSECORP MAINTAINED the best simulation system in the galaxy, in Sai's opinion. Any scenario he wanted to run, Sai could either build himself or request to be created for him by designers who knew how to mold virtual reality into the perfect play space. Sever mostly used the simulators to practice maneuvers, coordinated assaults and all that. Sai, though, preferred explosives testing. Playing out how various chemical and electrical setups would go boom, and whether the armor DefenseCorp provided could handle the resulting explosion.

Knowing he could set off, and survive, a bomb gave Sai one hell of a surprise to spring.

So when the skiff crunched and crashed into the tower, when Sai felt metal bars, flaked dry wall, and debris that defied description plaster against him, he knew his armor could handle it. Anything short of sustained laser fire or diamond-bladed weapons would have a tough time getting through to him.

The armor, though, did nothing to halt momentum.

The skiff finally hit something stronger than its sputtering bulk as it broke through the bay, into a wide corridor and against the wall behind. While the wall's outer shell collapsed, the skiff's busted front end stuck, sending Sai and Eponi flying forward through the space that had been occupied by the pilot house's roof. Sai didn't have the requisite reflexes to capture Eponi in mid-air while maintaining any semblance of composure, so he flew out flailing before slamming down through a busted skiff deck-docking bay wall combo pack.

Heavy enough to keep on rolling, Sai flopped off of that mess and slid along with the rubble, on his back, towards the hole the skiff's dipping bow created as it completed its apocalyptic crash.

Around and above him dangled broken supporting beams, flaring wires and pipes draining who knew what. White and gray metals, dust, and tile hung in the air or fell with Sai. The impact jolted his senses, but Sai knew that if he fell down that hole, into whatever room lay beyond, he'd have a hard time getting back to Eponi. So he reached out, grabbed for whatever he could, and set the studs in his boots launching out, searching for grip.

Sai's boots found purchase first, and Sai realized his mistake as his suddenly-stuck feet pitched him up off the skiff's deck and threw him forward, slamming Sai chest-down on the very slope he'd just been riding, further scattering shards and junk everywhere. He added his own curses to the alarms ringing out around him. Couldn't think of a better time to rage against whatever divine malefactor had thrown Sai on this mission. At least the other Severs weren't seeing this.

His ankles, meanwhile, definitely were *feeling* this, and, with his boots locked, Sai's ankles protested supporting the man's entire weight. They cracked, they strained, and Sai couldn't find purchase on the debris-coated makeshift ramp to push himself up. Two choices: either plunge ahead, or stay and break his ankles.

Sai took the plunge. Sucked in the studs on his boots, which popped free to his ankle's immense relief, and Sai slid into the ragged hole like the galaxy's clumsiest diver. The fall lasted two heartbeats, maybe three, before Sai banged into a floor made of much stronger stuff than the one he'd just fallen through. Softer material as well, which cushioned the impact enough for Sai to feel only a couple ribs crack, a weird twinge in his hip, and a bone-rattling bang to his skull. That latter blow kept Sai on the ground, fogging up his mind with dark clouds.

His helmet yelled at him, flashing alarms blaring on his visor, but Sai shut his eyes. Tried to ignore them for a long moment and splayed out on the floor. If whomever owned this placed wanted to take him prisoner, Sai would go. Just to make the craziness end. He'd been on plenty of missions with Sever and most went sideways at one point or another, but crashing a skiff into a giant building on an unknown, yellow gas-covered swamp world? Something about that confluence broke Sai's composure. He needed a minute to get it back.

Sai's helmet did not give him that minute.

The alerts ticked up in tone and frequency, blasting into Sai's concussed ear drums until he managed to mutter the command to cut them off. That utterance and the slim connection with reality it provided proved enough for Sai to force his eyes back open. Stare sideways through the visor and its warnings. In bold red along the right side of his vision, the hard glass displayed a deep blue circle with a green dot in the middle—Sai—and a red dot trio steadily closing. Whether they meant Sai actual harm or not the armor wouldn't know, but in this place Sai could assume they weren't friends.

No rest for Severs.

Sai pushed, stood with a wavering weakness that had him shuffling from one foot to another, unsteady. The spacious room, lit in soft purple hues like a bad night club, spread up and around him. Odd shapes sat around, too. Big boulders, and what appeared to be fake trees, tall and shadowed, built right into the floor. Like someone had created an obstacle course, or a battlefield. And those red dots?

Not rocks. Not trees.

Sai shook his head, tried to figure out what he was looking at. His visor declared one of those red dots stood front and center, but to Sai, what came towards him looked more like the shivering hulk of a frozen giant. Humanoid, sure, but at least three meters tall, with a stretched face and blue-tinted limbs with all the wrong proportions. Gray hair clumped around the creature in various places, as if it suffered from a disastrous attempt to shave itself. No clothes, no weapons, but it moved towards Sai with a steady shamble.

"What are you?" Sai said, and he tried to back-step, to buy some distance, but his blurred brain sent him stumbling back instead.

Something grabbed him, held fast until Sai kicked his feet into a boost, which sent him flying a few meters away into another hard, painful impact with the floor. Looking back, Sai had a hard time focusing, but the thing that'd grabbed him looked tar black, sturdy. Also humanoid, but compact. Glistening in the violet light.

Sai looked towards the last red dot and was not surprised to find it, too, looked like a person, only one covered in mossy black-green growths. Arms and legs over-taken by quivering biological bulbs that made its every step towards Sai a squishy one. The third creature also completed Sai's unifying theme for the trio:

They were all damn ugly.

This time, when Sai stood, the shakes weren't so bad. His nose still seemed to smell something strange, and Sai's chest stabbed with the kind of pain that demanded urgent attention, but, for now, his body could rise to the moment. His hands, too—they drew his sword from Sai's back, where it'd ridden out the crash and subsequent slip'n'slide without issue.

As the three things converged on Sai, he held the blade out before him, its edge catching the light. Beautiful, really. If Sai was going to die in this tower, and he had no doubt people would kill him when this ended, then he hoped some video of this would make it out. Launch across the galactic airwaves to his family, so his son and daughter would get one good heroic picture of their dad.

Then, raising the blade to his right shoulder, Sai nodded at the three creeping monsters, and went to work.

TWENTY-EIGHT

Dirty Work

THE ASTEROID MINERS were one of two attitudes. You didn't save the guy in trouble, because his own mistakes had probably put him there. Why risk yourself to save someone from his own failure? The other perspective said to dive in, do whatever you could to save the miner because tomorrow it might be you that needed the saving, and help tended to come around. Gregor preferred to split the difference and weed out the worthless chaff before they could be in a position to hurt themselves or anyone else.

When he made it to DefenseCorp, that attitude endeared him to approximately nobody. Who wanted a squad-mate that would judge your fitness for the position and, based on their own opinion, decide whether or not to help you? Gregor's testing, his field performance, who he sat with in the mess hall, all coalesced around his brutal effectiveness and zero tolerance for subpar companions. He'd happily take on long odds, so long as the fighter by his side was as good, or nearly so, as Gregor.

Until Medux Prime.

Relegated to patrol duty after alienating his fellows on

Roast, Gregor had been swapped into a D-grade unit meant to keep a bunch of hapless civilians from killing each other as Medux Prime's giant waves crashed its far smaller islands around its surface and into one another. Any sane human would have declared the planet uninhabitable, but the species that'd grown up there thrived on conflict, and extracted a whole lot of amazing gemstones created by big old rocks slamming into each other again and again.

Gregor had spent two years riding those islands, and in that time he'd worked with the dregs of the dregs. People DefenseCorp stashed on Medux Prime not because they had Gregor's personality problems, but because they barely knew which end of a rifle to point at the enemy.

Surrounded by fools, and regarded as such by a commander whose sole objective seemed to be skimming enough precious stones for himself to retire, Gregor learned to . . . teach. Learned to accept it when a rookie incited a riot by accidentally threatening a newly-smashed island's leaders. Learned to jump in and help when a new arrival put their armor on backwards, triggered their boosters, and sent themselves flying into the sea.

Eventually, with his ragtag DefenseCorp failures, Gregor confronted Medux Prime's commander. He strode into the man's office, hammer in his hands, and demanded the commander stop stealing from the aliens paying DefenseCorp to keep them and their gems safe. When the commander laughed in his face, Gregor had gestured out to the squad of, if not hardened, then not totally inept soldiers behind him. The commander paled, declared he'd stop, and then promptly reassigned them all, ditching Gregor in Sever, where the hammer-wielding man would never get near Medux Prime again.

Still, Gregor considered it a moral victory.

So when he saw Rovo, the rookie, maybe dead but maybe alive in that awful sludge, Gregor had climbed halfway over the edge before Aurora gave him the go-ahead to dive. Gregor slotted back his hammer as he leapt off the platform—the falling smash was among his favorite moves, but crushing an already enveloped Rovo seemed like a poor choice—and plummeted into the muck. Unlike the creatures he'd mashed and then burned in the room below, whose skin had been overgrown with this stuff, the pure filth had a lighter feel to it. Like moving through thick spiderwebs, albeit ones fine leaving a liquid stain. Gregor's weight alone sunk him to his waist, but a quick fire from his boot boosters pushed Gregor back to the top with a fantastic gunk spray, where he could kneel and stay, with slight impressions, on the surface.

"All right?" Aurora said, their near-field transmission bringing her voice to Gregor's ear as if they stood next to each other.

"Alive, but it's grabbing at me," Gregor said, peeling himself away from the clutching strands and making his way over to Rovo. "Might need help getting the rookie out."

"Let's see if our friend has any ideas."

Gregor didn't wait for Felix. Once he made it to Rovo's sole sticking limb, Gregor gave the blue-plated boot a tug, solving nothing. He couldn't get much leverage with the sloshing filth, and Gregor felt an opposing pull too—something wanted Rovo to stay down there.

The muck decided it wanted Gregor too.

Black and green tendrils rose from the goop, stretching towards Gregor like snakes from a swamp. He batted at them with one hand, while continuing to pull at Rovo with the other, but the swats did nothing to deter the reaching things. They didn't even try to dodge, just took Gregor's hits, splattered and reformed back for more. A couple slipped past on the left side, where Gregor was tugging, and a sudden yellow fire burst torched them away.

"Covering you," Aurora said. "Focus on getting Rovo out. Felix says he can't control it."

"Throw him in, see if that gives him any ideas."

Gregor needed a switch in strategy. He looked behind him, to the ladder climbing out of the muck towards the top. It looked sturdy, maybe strong enough to hold his weight. Gregor let Rovo go, reached his hands to his waist and popped the pair of link lines, like the ones Sai had used to get beneath the mine outside, and stuck them to Rovo's boot. Designed to keep people together in vacuum, Gregor figured the cables would be able to handle the stress.

Whether Rovo's bones would survive without breaking, well, better than being dead.

As Aurora stitched golden fire around him, turning tendrils to burning ash, Gregor lurched back to the ladder, gripped it with both hands and climbed. Once he'd made it up a couple of rungs, Gregor felt hard yanks on the lines as laser fire torched close. Aurora had to protect the lines too, now, with the tendrils getting their slimy tentacles on the links.

Aurora had to be spending too much rifle power on this, but Sever missions never went right, always swerved sideways. Maximum risk, maximum excitement.

"Hang on, rookie," Gregor said, broadcasting the words on the squad's channel. Rovo might be able to hear, might be able to get ready. "And if you can hear me, push."

Gregor tried a step, strained against the lines. Pressed with his feet, pulled with his hands, and strained against the muck's grip. With a sucking, curdling sound, the dark surface parted and Rovo's leg squeezed out, rips spreading and repairing in the muck. Now that he had momentum, Gregor kept going. One step after another, sweat forming and pouring at the effort despite the armor's attempt to keep Gregor at optimal temps. Tendrils jumped at Rovo's body and Aurora shot them back, stitching such a constant assault that a growing fire started, burning the ample living matter.

Heroic actions deserved heroic backdrops.

With Rovo's limp, sludge-coated body now resting on the fiery surface, Gregor looked back up towards the platform and made a rough calculation. Gregor bent his knees on the ladder, let go with his hands and jumped, pushed just clear of the next rung. He kicked in his boosters, depleting their batteries to zero, which punched Gregor up the last few meters until Rovo's weight killed the ascent. Gregor snatched the next to last rung on the ladder, banged his knees against the wall, and glanced down to see Rovo hanging, helmet down. But the rookie was off the surface, free from the tendrils.

Another lunge had Gregor over the lip, and Aurora came over to help, pulling on the links. Felix, Gregor noted, had been stashed back in his hovel, the creature's blue eyes staring out at them.

"He gave up?" Gregor asked as they reeled Rovo in.

"Didn't want to get shot," Aurora replied, then took a look over the edge. "Looks like I started a fire."

"Let it burn."

Aurora didn't answer that, just kept huffing and pulling. Gregor couldn't see any reason to save the sludge, living or not. Felix had almost killed Rovo, had tried to kill the two of them, and this growing grime seemed to be on his side. It ought to be destroyed.

Rovo came over the platform's edge, his armor marred

with pits, as if the slime had been dissolving its way through. The rookie's visor showed cracks and clouded sections where it'd done its level best to resist the acid. A red line trickled down from Rovo's forehead, too. A gash from a fall, most likely. Still, the armor reported Rovo's overall vitals were good. The rookie lived, even if he wasn't conscious.

"Time for the ugly one to go," Gregor said, unlinking himself from Rovo and pointing at Felix. "Any final words, monster?"

"I have plenty," Felix said, scrunching further back into his hole. "Plenty I could tell you, too, about this place."

"Not interested," Gregor replied, but as he went towards Felix, Aurora grabbed his arm.

"I want to know," Aurora said. "Record what he says. It might be valuable for us."

Two ways to take that word, valuable. Intel on the enemy always had value, could save lives or make the mission easier. Or make money. Why Aurora would care about money at this stage, with more than half the squad wounded or missing, made no sense. But then, Gregor wasn't the commander. Didn't have to report back to DefenseCorp about the mission's success and failure. He would rather smash Felix right there with the hammer, but if Aurora commanded, Gregor would obey.

"Talk, creature." Gregor crouched and glared, through his visor, at Felix.

As backdrops go, the burning bio-matter provided enough thick black smoke that the room's vents had to whir and churn to keep air flowing. Gregor's voice came over their relentless spin, punctuated by pops as bigger growths below burned and popped. Air filters kept some charred smell from leaking through into Gregor's armor, but not all, and someone less used to the smell of acrid mud might have choked on what leaked in. Still, Felix didn't flinch and he had no filter, no visor.

Gregor could show no weakness.

So Felix spoke, and they listened as the creature of Dynas revealed its secrets.

TWENTY-NINE

Desperate Times

SHE'D CRASHED FOUR TIMES. The first three had been minor ones, the accidents any racer was bound to run into. Karts, skiffs, whatever, they all had a thousand parts and if too many of them failed when Eponi yanked the craft through a tight turn in the massive, curling vines on Kantos, or dove beneath a boulder spray from the stone geysers on Ferra, she'd wind up splattering into a wall and depending on her bubble to survive. A nigh impenetrable sphere around a kart's cockpit and a racing skiff's pilot house, the bubbles were great at keeping racers alive. Eponi would have loved one now, except the Thissalids, who held the secret to the bubble's manufacture, only provided them to racers because of the species's overriding obsession with the sport.

Then again, Eponi couldn't hate on the Thissalids. Without them, space racing wouldn't exist like it did. Too many deaths, too few willing to throw long-lived lives on the line for too little cash. Make the racer almost invincible, though, and suddenly you had thrill-seekers eager to race through the wider galaxy.

Eponi didn't have a bubble when the skiff crashed on Dynas. She had Sai, and while the his armor did an admirable job keeping Eponi alive through the initial seconds when, with her eyes closed and head buried between Sai's limbs, Eponi felt the roaring heat, smelled the burning wires, and heard what sounded like a thousand instruments breaking at once, Eponi would have far preferred the silver invulnerability net.

Especially when the second impact, when the skiff broke through the corridor, sent them both flying, with Sai's far heavier bulk launching away from her. Eponi bounced off the breaking wall, just to the left of where the skiff had made its opening and through which it continued to slide. She caromed to the floor, rolling with the momentum and feeling every moment she touched, well, anything.

Human bodies, turned out, weren't meant to ricochet.

Clarity came in brief whiffs as Eponi lay flat on the floor. Sparks showered around her, providing little burning bursts to distract her from the more serious scrapes and cuts. Her head hurt where something, jagged metal, maybe, had caught her hair and sliced it away, leaving a barren patch on her head's right side. Blood, which looked black before Eponi realized it was collecting ash and dirt on its way down her face, trickled onto the floor around her.

Eponi thought crashing the skiff would be their only chance at survival, but she might've killed them both anyway. At least Sai might survive in his armor. Eponi? Eponi was toast.

Until the sprinklers activated, coupled with a thick powder meant to kill electrical fires. The foamy stuff rained down from above, splashing all over her and the wreckage behind. It washed away her blood, cleaned out the tatters in her skin suit, and, with the water's harsh cold, kept Eponi from breaking. She stood on an edge, and to one side lay all the problems, the terrible choices and unlucky moments that'd brought her to this point, and on the other . . . on the other was movement. She could go forward and hope things went better. Trust her skills, her body not to totally break down.

Aurora would be yelling at her to get up now. Tell her that Eponi was missing her moment, lying here in the growing puddle. Say that Eponi was hurting the squad by staying still.

She raced for herself, but, more and more as Eponi improved, for her team. The sponsors and the crew that put together her karts before every race, that kept her on time and on schedule hopping around the galaxy. She'd picked herself up after the crashes, the losses, and kept going.

Sever needed her. And what was this crash, really? A cut or two? Hair that would grow back? She'd had worse. She'd probably *have* worse on Dynas, given how terrible this place seemed to be.

"Not dying here," Eponi said the words without really meaning to, but they worked.

In the pouring sprinkler rain, she rose. Looked back towards the skiff as it slid through its hole and into the other room, disappearing. She'd have yelled for Sai except the tower's locals had begun to respond. Calls for help, for fire crews went out over the tower's, or at least this floor's, loudspeakers. Help would be coming, and Eponi didn't want to be here when they arrived.

She walked, limping as her left leg didn't quite feel up to things yet, away from the wreck. The corridor, aside from the sprinklers and foam, paid homage to the tried and true design sensibilities of sterile interplanetary corporations: Soft walls made to look metallic, with few pictures but signage and monitors aplenty showing this and that status report. Despite living in an age where information could be at anyone's fingertips, the overall trend seemed to be to put data everywhere else too. Rather than art, why not have something useful, like an event calendar or the latest update to your vacation policy?

Eponi did, though, find one helpful sign amid the mess: lavatory.

Running the racing circuit, Eponi had established a universal constant as she crossed between worlds: the toilets always changed. Sometimes, depending on the species controlling the place, toilets didn't even exist and any humans had to use pop-up varieties that supplied convenience at comfort's cost. Here, on Dynas, Eponi had mixed expectations. On one side, Dynas sat so far outside the populous belt, with so little ship traffic, that holding out hope for a luxurious lavatory seemed naive. On the other, the tower they'd landed in clearly had a lot of cash poured into it. Techno features like a full landing bay and multi-fire extinguishing systems spoke to a care in design. Given her current condition, Eponi wanted, demanded, dreamed of something better than a hole in the ground.

What she got when she stepped through the human-sized door—an indicator, like with the guards, that whomever bankrolled this place was not into aliens—was something else altogether.

The hallmarks of a galactic-standard bathroom were there: stalls, anti-bacterial stations, and eye-activated cleansing washes. Joining them, though, were blackish green mold gobs on the walls, while floor sections looked like ash-coated feet had walked there. The counter's left side, meant for cosmetic adjustments, had broken away, ice-white fringes coating the rubbled edge. Yellowed light flowed from ceiling-length diodes above, and someone had placed scent-pouring nodes in the corners that gave off a strong lavender.

"What the hell?" Eponi muttered as she stepped inside, as she leaned down and confirmed nobody sat inside the two stalls.

Dynas, man. What a world.

Eponi went to the cleansers first and starting wiping and washing off her cuts, the grime and gunk. The water, at least, came through clear and cool. Felt nice between the stings as she swabbed on the anti-bacterial gel. When she finished, Eponi still looked haggard—her torn uniform and red lines criss-crossing her skin did her no favors—but now the pain wasn't amplified by the crash's confusing, dirty aftermath.

Now what to do about the rest of the place? What was growing in here? What had cracked the counter and blackened the floor's tiles?

Either whomever built this place had some strange design sensibilities, or something was wrong on Dynas.

A bigger problem than that mystery, though, lay in what Eponi herself was going to do. With a shredded, non-Dynas uniform, Eponi wouldn't get very far without being noticed, arrested, and probably, given the lovely reception Sever had received since hitting Dynas' airspace, shot. Stealth would be the way to play this one. Get some cover, see what happened to Sai, and try to figure out how to get back off world.

If Aurora and the rest of them found the VIP, maybe Eponi could pick them up on the way out. If they didn't, well, Eponi would still get away. Make it out alive. The mission had clearly gone sideways, and nothing in Defense-Corp's guidelines required suicidal devotion to the cause. Maybe DefenseCorp would even reward Eponi for coming back with intelligence, send in an army next time to get the job done.

Eponi went into one of the stalls, shut the door loosely and then stood on the toilet. Handicap bars gave Eponi something to hold on to, adjust her position to keep her legs rested while she waited. As traps went, this wasn't the most original, but Sever members had to learn fast to work with what they had.

"I know it's under control," the woman, sounding chilled, spoke as she came through the lavatory's door some minutes later—Eponi hadn't bothered tracking time, her exhaustion's steady growth served well enough. "Keep this whole floor closed until we've cleared it. I'll be out in a minute."

While Eponi couldn't see her, the woman did exactly what Eponi had—gone to the cleansers. Started up the water. Eponi held her breath still, shifted her feet. She'd spring out, crash the woman's head against the counter and then take, hopefully, the uniform. She hoped the woman had her size, or something close to it, or things would still be awkward.

Then the woman started to cry. The soft tears Eponi herself knew from those moments where things just seemed so absurdly wrong that she wondered how she ever came to be there, when life needed a reset.

A private cry could do that. A boost for the moment.

And good cover for a quick-step out of the lavatory.

Eponi made it through the door, had her hand reaching for the woman's throat before she stopped.

Couldn't help it. Couldn't tear her eyes away.

The woman, who didn't look much older than Eponi herself, who was gaunt to a worrying degree, clutched the counter with both of her hands. A purple uniform hung loose on her body, seeping into black boots designed to clutch difficult ground—strange in a techno-tower like this —but none of that held Eponi's focus like the right half of the woman's hair. Blue-white, like the frosted edge of a flower, the hair curled, fixed, while the left half was brown and straight. The woman's skin undercut what could have been a unique fashion choice, with the same blue-white cutting out patches.

A disease, maybe? Either way, Eponi froze at the strange sight, and the woman noticed her in the mirror.

"You're not touched," the woman said, not turning from the counter, her eyes tracking Eponi's in the mirror, widening as they took into account Eponi's obvious battering. "Wait."

"I'll kill you if you scream," Eponi said quick, snapping back to the moment. Diseased or no, Eponi couldn't let the woman summon help. "I need your uniform. With or without hurting you in the process."

The woman, with the cleansing water continuing to wash over her hands, took a deep breath. "Of course the one fighting downstairs wouldn't be the only person on the skiff. Where did you come from?"

She seemed far too calm. Didn't respect Eponi's threat. Time to change that.

"Last chance," Eponi said, loading as much threat into her voice as she could. "Uniform, now."

This time the woman turned around. Started undoing the series of buttons holding the uniform together, "Are you from Dynas somewhere? Did they keep some of you hidden?"

"Hidden?" Eponi couldn't resist, and the woman seemed to be following her directions anyway.

The woman squinted as she lifted off the uniform's top. The skin-suit underneath gave Eponi more questions. High-quality mesh, with thermal regulators and vitals monitors woven in, suits like this were meant for settlers pushing on to new worlds or going to live in harsh environments. Dynas, with its ready supply of oxygen and within-normal-range gravity, wouldn't have warranted this kind of gear.

"You're not off-world, are you?" the woman asked. "You couldn't be."

Eponi ignored that, focused instead on an earlier word, "You said touched a minute ago. What did you mean? Is that what's going on with your . . . body?"

"So innocent," the woman said, stepping out of the uniform's bottom pants, which had the pocket multitude someone working in maintenance might need. Eponi noticed the woman didn't remove any of the ID tags sticking to the cloth. "It will find you soon, I'm sure. It passes to everyone now. The only question is which one you'll be."

The woman folded her arms, waited for Eponi to put on the uniform.

"I don't understand?" Eponi said. "What are you talking about?"

"Be careful," the woman replied with a quick laugh. "Once Anaskya finds you, you'll look like me."

"Anaskya?"

"This is what desperation does," the woman said, hand reaching up to her hair. "She's infecting whomever she wants now. I don't know why I'm telling you this, except, I suppose, it doesn't matter. You're going to die, just like the rest of us."

"Noted." Eponi struck quick with her right hand, a crack to the woman's temple that sent her falling to the floor.

Eponi caught the woman with her left hand at the last second, lowering the unconscious body softly to the tiles and, in the process, getting plenty of blue-white gunk on her left hand. Eponi cursed, ran her hands under the cleansing water, then slipped on the uniform. A little large for her, but it'd pass a cursory inspection. Plenty of tools inside too, in case Eponi felt the need to get mechanical. With her weapons lost in the crash, at least she had a microlaser now. Could give someone a nice little burn if they came after her.

Outside the lavatory, Eponi pressed back through the people, soldiers, engineers, whomever crushing towards the crash. After the woman, Eponi started noticing patches and discolorations here and there. To various degrees, plenty appeared infected. Great. So not only was she alone, cut off without any radio contact with her squad, Eponi was in the middle of a disease-ridden enclave. She jammed her hands in her pockets and tried not to touch anyone, an exercise she failed continuously as she pressed through hallways until she made it to the floor's central lobby. Goal one was to find some sort of breathing mask, goal two was to get out of this tower, and goal three? Get off-world by any means necessary.

A spacious, circular room with several different lifts and a gigantic piece of ceiling artwork displaying what looked like a watercolor version of a bacterial cell, the room spaced the other art—all cellular depictions—on its walls with monitors displaying alerts, orders, and in one case, a live video feed showing someone Eponi knew. Sai. Still in his armor, the demolitionist swung his blade in quick slashes, cutting through things that looked like humans, but at the same time definitely were not. Looking at the screen from behind a crowd of other people, Eponi couldn't quite make out what the things were, but it seemed like a whole lot of them were shambling towards Sai now.

"What's going on?" Eponi ventured to ask the person

in front of her, a shorter man whose neck was all black and green, bubbling a little at the nape.

"That guy crashed with the skiff, fell right into the testing block," the man answered without turning around. "Looks like we're going to let him waste all the failures before we cleanse the room. Solves the problem for the ones who didn't want to push the button themselves, I guess."

Eponi started to ask what cleansing the room meant, then stopped herself. Too many people around here, and one of them might wonder why Eponi didn't know something she should. So instead she backed away from the crowd, looked over at the lifts. If Sai had fallen down a floor, maybe Eponi could get to him, let him out. Of course, that would mean risking herself, risking goal number one.

Sever squad, always making her life difficult.

THIRTY

Family Dinner Dreams

Rovo WAITED till his entire family sat down at the table, an old oak number that his parents insisted upon despite new models that could keep the same appearance with far less upkeep. His father set plates thick with pasta down at each of the five places, and his mother opened the sparkling wine with that satisfying pop coming from the tiny, embedded speaker in the bottle's seal. A perfect setting: the whole family back for dinner, Rovo on his only planetside visit of the year. Even Tau's indifferent weather had decided to cooperate, leaving a silver sky with the planet's rings making a fuzzy white slash through the center clear through the porch's glass ceiling. They all wore summer clothes, basked in the dry air and smiled as Rovo prepped to break the news that he'd never see them again.

DefenseCorp had a script for this, one that'd been refined over too many decades filled with children telling parents, wives telling husbands, or multicellular organisms explaining to their hive minds why they were going to be gone soon. Why they'd be sent across the galaxy to points where communication would occur over years rather than seconds. Why relationships would be put on pause, possibly forever, in the name of adventure, in the name of noble pursuits, in the name of peace and prosperity.

Rovo read it word for word—DefenseCorp's contract required this, and Rovo had to record the whole thing so the script and its reaction could be studied, refined even further—and by the end, when he closed with the line preaching to some higher ideal, his father shook his head and his mother started to laugh in that heartless way she had whenever one of her children, in her opinion, was making a terrible mistake. His sisters, one of whom kept eating throughout the speech, reacted with indifference. Rovo couldn't be too shocked at that. As the oldest, he'd disappeared to his DefenseCorp space station assignment over Tau years ago and missed a lot of their lives.

To them, Rovo was probably a ghost figure already. One who showed up once a year, who said nothing about his job—almost all communication Rovo dealt with had security seals—and had no connection with their town, their planet anymore.

"So you're gonna go die somewhere far away, never see us again, for what?" his dad said, finally.

"Because I can't do this anymore," Rovo said, turning off the DefenseCorp recorder he'd placed on the table prior to the speech. "I can't sit in that station reading messages all day, every day, until I die in a few centuries."

"Oh yes, poor you," his mother said. Rovo admired the way his parents could effortlessly tag-team their admonishment, each one driving in their own nails. "Such a terrible job you have, with security, free rent up there. Most of us on Tau have to fight to keep the robots from taking our places, but you're too good for that."

"Yes, mother, I am too good for it." Rovo had already decided on this tack. Stick up for his life, his desires.

"DefenseCorp cleared me for this, and I'm going to take them up on the offer."

"So you're trading your family for cash," his father said.

"I'm living my life."

Other than his sisters, none of them had touched the immaculate meal yet. They all stared at it, quiet.

Then a dark green, black blob plopped into Rovo's plate, dead center. Sauce splattered. Rovo blinked. Where'd that come from? He looked up, but his parents hadn't noticed. His sisters kept eating, shoveling fork-fulls of the spaghetti into their mouths as if they'd been starved. His parents stared, vacant-eyed at their own dishes.

"Mom?" Rovo asked as another moldy glob fell from above and splashed into the middle of the table.

She didn't respond, and Rovo looked up, towards the glass ceiling and that beautiful sky. Bubbling mold covered the glass, now. Tendrils grew down towards him, reaching and looking like living tornadoes as they spiraled. Rovo tried to stand up, get away from the table, but he couldn't. He felt cold sludge on his feet, his arms, locking him into the chair. Rovo looked back to his parents, tried to open his mouth to call for help, but the mold had found its way there too, crawling over his face, inside his mouth. The black fell on his parents, covering them.

His sisters kept eating, even as the mold overtook their bodies, as it covered Rovo's eyes and banished him to darkness.

Rovo's eyes shot open and he saw blood, tasted it. Above him, through his red-smeared visor, were industrial lights, not a mold-coated sky. Though these lights seemed really hazy. Smoke. Thick smoke. But when Rovo breathed, he inhaled none of it. His heart beat, and while he tasted the bloody trickle coming into his mouth, Rovo could open it. Could move his arms and legs.

"Back with us?" Aurora asked, her face coming into view. "First time getting shock-jocked?"

Rovo limped through a nod, a feeble move but all he could do.

"Gregor pulled you out of that pit," Aurora continued. "It's on fire now, and I'm going to need you to get moving so we don't burn."

"Okay, I'm, uh, I'm getting up," Rovo said, but Aurora had already pulled away.

The rookie rose to a sitting position, trying to comprehend what Aurora had just told her, and came face-to-face with the hunched, ice-eyed and sludge-covered creature that'd led Rovo all the way in. Shock-jock tech was designed to pull someone out of their own unconscious before they would awake naturally. Hard-hitting stuff, and not healthy. That Rovo had to experience it at all came down to this guy right here. Rovo reached for his pistol, but found an empty holster instead.

Then strong arms lifted Rovo up until he stood, looking down at Felix.

"I said get moving," Aurora spoke behind Rovo. "Gregor's already heading out to make sure the hallway's clear."

"But this thing, he's what led me into—he pushed me in!"

"Rookie, when I give you an order, I expect you to obey." Aurora pointed Rovo out the door, away from the smoke. "Go."

Rovo shot one last glare at the fungus man, but left. Aurora seemed like a leader that would tolerate a question or two, but when it came time to blitz it, other opinions weren't an option. Instead, Rovo went after Gregor, unarmed and with his armor creaking every step of the way. He brushed at the leftover bits of mold, and wondered if he'd made the right call, or if this would get him killed, just as his father predicted.

That dream. It'd been so close to the real thing. So close. If he died, is that where he'd go?

Rovo saw Gregor not far ahead, at the triple-hallway intersection. Wondered if Gregor ever thought about what'd happen when he died. Maybe he'd go to some fantasy land where Gregor could swing that hammer all day long.

While Rovo would watch mold devour his family time and time again.

THIRTY-ONE

The Master Plan

AURORA PULLED Felix with her as she left the big, burning room. Shut the door. Either the base would figure out a way to put out the fire, or it wouldn't. Not Aurora's problem, but most definitely one for Felix.

The fungal man didn't fight back as Aurora dragged him along, her left hand pulling his mushy mass along the hallway floor. Though he'd been a chatterbox before, Felix fell silent now, having given up his secrets and placed himself firmly at Sever's mercy. A capitulation Aurora would have regarded with pitiless contempt, except she'd given Felix so much contempt already that heaping on more felt like a waste.

Exploitation. The word summed up both Felix and Dynas pretty well. A cast-off mire world made easy, through its watery life, to transform with massive seed dumps and far enough away from galactic traffic to do so with minimal interference.

Who would care enough to pay for a new world this far away? Felix didn't know, but whomever it was had no desire for Dynas itself. They wanted all the other worlds, the ones left behind because their atmospheres weren't good enough, their biospheres were too hostile, or some other reason that turned the profit/loss equation upside down and left them bereft of corporate colonization.

Terraforming planets cost cash, took most of a life's few centuries to do. Transforming a person . . . Aurora had to figure that could be done much faster. You'd have a lot of accidents on the way, but if you wanted to exploit resources within decades instead of centuries, fit the people to the planet. Dynas became the incubator. Felix and most everyone else here, the test subjects. Proofs of concept.

Spin up a core city on Dynas for the initial testing, then send the viable subjects to control spokes where they could be monitored. Perfected and controlled. Then, once you had a viable specimen that retained all their human intelligence but with the physical attributes to survive on a new planet, you made more. Manufactured them, really. Traffic in the desperate, scheme them away from their homes with lies and offers, and abandon them to the experiments. The potential profit off of a single success made the whole investment easy to excuse, terrible to acknowledge.

"Why are you different from the others?" Aurora said as she dragged Felix along. The one hole in Felix's story came from his own part in it, how he'd managed to get so much influence over the base when he was, by his own admission, one of these experiments. "If you can even call them that."

"Luck." Felix muttered, wet and sloppy. "Genetic lottery. I don't know. For our group, they brought us out here if we lived more than a month after the first infection. So we wouldn't get contaminated by anything else."

Up ahead, at the triple intersection with the hallways, Gregor and Rovo held watch. As Aurora approached, she waved them on. Scouts against whomever might be left here. Things had gone quiet since they'd come up for Felix, and Aurora wondered whether Sai and Eponi had killed or drawn all the other guards away. That neither Sever member had shown up yet bothered her, but without any bodies, she'd assume they were alive.

"Once here you stayed in one of those rooms down-stairs or in a smaller cell while they kept eyes on you. All the time poking, prodding, measuring," Felix sputtered. He'd started to move under his own power now, but slow enough that Aurora still gave him the tug-along treatment. "When it takes you, and it takes almost everyone, eventually, I don't know if I can describe it."

"Looks awful."

"Yes. But it feels different. Like growing up, maybe. Where you feel new things, but also still yourself?"

"You're not convincing me that what you've gone through is puberty 2.0."

"No, but we aren't dead. What you burned in there, those were my friends. People I had come here with, suffered with, hoped with."

Aurora stopped. Pushed Felix back against the hallway wall, put her right hand on her pistol but didn't draw it. "You dragged Rovo to that room. You trapped Gregor and I. All of this is your fault. So stop whining and keep talking. Maybe you'll find a reason we should let you live."

Cash by copious amounts would suffice, and if Felix had it right about an operation this big, DefenseCorp would pay Sever tons of cash for the contracts Defense-Corp would get to clean the mess up. But Felix didn't need to know that, and if he had further gems to give away, Aurora wanted to hear them.

"That's the problem they have," Felix said, Aurora still holding him to the wall, though the fungal man didn't seem afraid. "They change us through a virus, but the virus wants to spread. It wants to keep growing. My body happens to keep it under control, most don't. If they can't, the virus eats them unless it can find new hosts to spread to."

"It would eat them anyway." Aurora had seen enough biological weapons to know they didn't play by simple rules. "You feeding us to those things wouldn't stop it."

"What can we do but delay the end?"

Aurora rolled her eyes, dropped Felix to the floor, "Guess what, Felix? Your end is here."

A virus meant to make people survive adverse conditions, but that really turned them into dying, disease bombs. Aurora could pitch that to DefenseCorp, and she'd snapped enough pictures with her helmet's embedded camera to prove it. No reason to let Felix and his bio-swarm survive, possibly infect someone else. Not what DefenseCorp paid them to do, but the occasional bit of charity towards the universe helped Aurora sleep at night.

"Should I protest?" Felix said, lingering where Aurora left him, limp and listless. "I can't beat you. I tried, failed. So you have every right to murder me."

"I do." Aurora, though, didn't shoot. She kept an ear out for Gregor and Rovo as they swept towards the lift, declared it clear. Something about Felix's voice, his general attitude, befuddled her anger. "I have every reason, every moral obligation to blow this base to dust."

"One base among many. Do you have the time, will you live long enough to wipe our stain clean?"

"Have to start somewhere."

"Then perhaps you don't start with me. With this place." Felix spread his blob arms. "I almost had it. Three guards had already fallen before you arrived. Give me this, my little sanctuary in the swamp, and I will give you the codes to their systems. You can go, find your friends, and leave me with mine."

"Our friends? You were lying?"

"Only slightly. The other two you came with embarked on a skiff some time ago. I don't know where they went, but they are not here."

Aurora considered. Trusting Felix seemed like a poor choice, given that he'd tried to kill them all. But his story had plausibility, and Felix had to know he'd get a swift end if he tried to trick them again. If they left Felix alive, too, Aurora could always come back later with a DefenseCorp bounty in hand, fulfill her earlier promise to herself and turn Felix into slag for a healthy profit.

The universe could wait.

"We're falling behind," Aurora said. "Talk as we go, Felix, and if your information is good, you and your disease might get to live after all."

THIRTY-TWO

The Swordmaster

THE LESSONS BEGAN on the wide balcony, before the fall. Ayami took Sai out there every morning when he was younger, then his teenage years pushed him away from his mother until that morning, as word spread that things weren't going very well for Vitas, the city-world they called home. Riots, lawlessness grew as those with the means fled the planet and those without burned it. Ayami and Sai, stuck in the middle, had to fend for themselves.

Ayami set the sheathed blade on a small glass table, the weapon long enough to hang over the table's edge and poke a shadow against the white stone floor. Today's sun— for simplicity's sake, Sai had learned, most human worlds referred to their life-giving stars as 'suns', whatever their technical name—rose on what would have been a beautiful morning across the world-spanning city, were it not for the black smoke rising among Vitas' towers.

"Is that from the wall?" Sai asked.

The sword had hung there all his life, a crown to a stacked shelf holding family heirlooms, non-digital pictures, and other relics that deserved some prominence in their small home. Seeing it now brought enough curiosity to kill Sai's general distrust towards anything his mother cared to have him do these days. Always chores, always preparing for the future, as if Vitas would survive this crisis and go on as it had before. As if Sai would follow in her footsteps and plop himself down at a computer every day forevermore.

"It is," Ayami replied. "Though it doesn't always stay there. Pick it up."

Watching his mom, wondering where the trick was, Sai lifted the sword from the table with both hands. Light, but with enough weight to feel solid. Sai held the sheath across both hands, cradling it like a gift.

"Take the sheath in your left hand, grip it here." Ayami pantomimed where, and Sai copied her motion. "Now draw the blade. Slow."

Sai did, felt the metal slide along a sheath made to fit. He stuck the blade twice on the first attempt—katanas, it turned out, were not malleable—but managed to clear the sheath with a flourish. The silver blade caught the sunlight, and as Sai looked along its sharp length, he could read names, a line from tip to hilt, ending with his mother's.

"You'll add your own, when you are ready," Ayama said, watching her son.

"When will that be?"

"A long time from now," Ayami replied. "Now, let me show you how to hold it so you don't hurt yourself. You can be a fool with your schooling and make out all right, but you cannot be a fool with this."

Sai couldn't read the names along the blade in the purple-dark room, but he knew them all by heart. The katana, now, bore multiple kills anyway, their leftovers coating it and Sai both. What had been a trio had become a dozen, and more continued leaching in from lifts in the floor; platforms that fell and rose up bearing more delirious, grasping enemies.

While the initial set had seemed as lost as zombies from old movies, the fresh arrivals were more coherent. They kept back from Sai's cuts, choosing to break off branches from the obstacles and throw them, or use other things as makeshift clubs. They yelled at him too, with snatches close to making sense, but most vanishing into watery gurgles or hoarse gasps. They may have been human once, but had transgressed into fallen things.

Every cut with the katana sapped Sai's strength ever so slightly, and his arms burned as he removed an ash-black head from another creature that had ventured too close. His helmet beeped a warning from behind, and Sai crouched, flipped the grip so the katana pointed behind him, and shoved his hands back, driving the blade deep. A jerk forward withdrew it, the katana catching on bone for a split second.

Four more, two blues, two greens, as Sai had started calling them, converged from the front. Aside from the creatures, the gaping hole in the room's roof and its myriad obstacles had stayed the same. No doors presented an escape, no demands to surrender had come from the tower's owners. Sai figured someone had to be throwing these hordes at him, but who? And why?

And would it continue until Sai could lift the sword no more?

He didn't relish that thought, so as the nearest four approached him, Sai swung the blade over his shoulder and slid it into the same sheathe his mother had laid on the table all those years ago, now bolted into his armor. Sai broke right, using a spindly tree to buy himself some separation as he clomped along the purple-black tiles. His pursuit shifted to follow him, wheeling about with unsteady shuffles. Clicks and chimes rang out as more lifts arrived, carrying yet more monsters. Sai could have expected the tower to have a limitless robot supply, but people?

As Sai jogged towards the right wall, he reached towards his chest and unbuckled a mine, leaving only two remaining. He flicked the mine behind him, towards the creatures, and dove forward, curling up into a ball. Generally, Sai loved explosions. Enjoyed the shockwave that came from a well-placed device, and the gaping destruction that followed. None of that joy came from being right next to the bomb as it went off.

The mine blew with frenetic force, the tiles conducting the rippling jolt like live wires and rattling Sai against the floor even as the hot waves cascaded over his armor. Sai blinked for a status readout, and his armor replied back that conditions were functional, though his boot boosters had shrapnel damage. Not a great outcome, but now, with any luck, Sai had a way out.

He straightened, stood, and counted another seven things creeping towards him from the room's farther edges. Sai also saw his mine, while charring a wide swath on the floor, had failed to excavate so much as a spoon's worth of tile for Sai to escape through. The demolition man wouldn't be blowing his way out of here.

Sai took a deep breath, settled into the inevitable and drew his sword again. His family's katana, with him to the end. Poetic, Sai supposed. He hoped someone filmed this last stand, blasted it out along the galaxy's network so his family could see what happened to him. That he'd gone down fighting.

Light flared from his left, along the near wall. Bright, Sai's helmet and his own pupils took a second to adjust to the glare, to register the figure standing in the doorway as

Eponi. Still without her armor, though wearing different clothes, she lived. She waved at him. She yelled something.

"What?" Sai shouted back, started going her way.

"Come on!" Eponi said. "Stop being slow!"

Just like her to keep up the insults, even now. Sai broke into a run, out-pacing the pursuit with the ease of an adult escaping a toddler swarm. The things were only frightening if you couldn't get away. Eponi stepped aside as Sai made it to the door, as he ran through into the next room. As he went under the threshold, the door slammed down behind him, sealing away the enemies.

And trapping him in with plenty more.

Waiting in the room, rifles raised, were at least a dozen guards. They had Sai surrounded, and as he turned right to Eponi, started to ask what was going on, his helmet flared an alarm. Another threat, from his left.

Sai never saw what hit him.

THIRTY-THREE

Comet Puncher

AURORA ASKED Gregor about the design after he ran it every day for a month. Gregor hadn't built a complicated scenario—he lacked both the skill and motivation for that —but rather a winding corridor series with pop-out hallways and doors for his demons to use, for them to appear as Gregor advanced and stomped his way through. The program built most of it, really, taking the data from images Gregor supplied, stills and videos from his home. The simulators were really good at extracting the details, modeling them into a virtual space. Gregor could put on the sim suit and step into Snowball, and then destroy it.

It'd been the latter element, steadily reducing Gregor's home to rubble, that had been flagged and reported Aurora's way. She sat him down late one night—a programmed day-night cycle existed for psychological reasons on the *Nautilus*—poured *Nautilus*-distilled whiskey into tumblers, and asked Gregor if he'd lost his mind.

"It's an itch I wanted to scratch," Gregor said, swallowing the offer in one go. The whiskey tasted like old iron. "Let me."

"DefenseCorp isn't a big fan of wild, homicidal impulses towards one's home," Aurora replied. "Looks bad for business if something like this gets out. Customers might think DefenseCorp is full of fuses like yours, waiting to blow."

"Do you think I'm a fuse?"

Three missions together, three since Gregor had joined Sever. All had been bloody, all had resulted in destructions warranted and unwarranted. All three were considered successful.

"You kept the hammer," Aurora sipped her own beverage, nursing it with the nonchalance of someone who could savor anything, no matter how terrible. "Why?"

"It's effective."

"Not because you want to murder your hometown with it?"

"I can't get back there," Gregor said. He picked up the glass, stared at its emptiness, till Aurora pulled the bottle from her pack and refilled it. "DefenseCorp won't take me."

"So you destroy it virtually instead."

"Therapy."

Aurora nodded, "Then do me a favor. Break things up. Keep Snowball to a once-a-week destruction, and I'll keep the red tape away from you."

GREGOR LET the rookie take the lead again as they swept back towards the lifts. There should have been heavy resistance by this point, but they encountered none. Even bodies left by previous encounters, like the set Aurora and Gregor smashed in their initial return through the lift, had disappeared. Stains remained, but no other evidence. Standing in the middle of what should have been a grisly site, Rovo looked over at Gregor and spread his hands.

"I don't know," Gregor answered the gesture. "They should be here."

Aurora and Felix came up behind them, making it three armored mercenaries and one diseased mutant. Not exactly the makeup Gregor wanted, but it would suffice.

"I didn't think they would actually leave," Felix said, seeing the stains.

"What do you mean?" Gregor asked him.

"I made a deal," Felix replied. "Told them we would devour all of you in exchange for peace. They think we're going to die anyway out here so they left."

"Why would they trust you?" Aurora said.

"I used to be one of them, remember?" Felix went over to the lift, pushed the call button. "Just because I look like this doesn't mean I've changed how I think."

Gregor watched Aurora, waited for the signal. He could crush Felix right now, and it wouldn't take more than a second's effort. His commander didn't give the sign. She waited until the lift opened, and then Aurora ordered the two of them inside of it.

"You're leaving him alive?" Rovo asked as Gregor entered the lift. "How? Isn't he the enemy?"

"Follow the orders," Gregor said. While he wanted to hear her reasoning, worthy commanders like Aurora deserved to have their orders obeyed without hesitation. Questioning could come later, in private. "Get in."

"No," Rovo replied, as Felix turned between him and Aurora. "Not until I understand why we're not killing him for what he did to me. For what he tried to do to you."

"Because he's going to die anyway," Aurora said. "Felix bought himself some time by giving me the tram codes. Without them, we'd be stuck here. DefenseCorp won't let him live once we tell them what's happening anyway."

The rookie glared at Felix, "Guess that's what you deserve."

"Rookie. Now." Gregor clapped the hammer against his hands for emphasis, and Rovo took the hint, getting into the lift.

Aurora joined them and, with Felix giving a cold smile, the doors shut.

"How do you know he's not lying to you?" Rovo asked as the lift started its descent.

"Could be," Aurora replied. "If the codes don't work, we go back and stomp him. If they do, then Felix pays his price later."

"Focus, rookie," Gregor said. "Vengeance is a distraction."

Rovo stayed quiet after that. The lift hit the basement and together the three went towards the tram. Boarded it, and Aurora punched in the codes in the console towards the tram's front. Gregor took a seat where he'd have the best look as the tram went backwards along the track. A good chance to spot disaster before it struck.

When the mag-lev started humming, Gregor could feel the vibration. The pull stabilized soon enough, and as the tram began to pull away, the sensation vanished altogether. As if they were floating, the tram took them down a long tunnel leading to who knew where.

THE SIMULATORS MODELED Gregor's bedroom perfectly. The cramped space served for sleeping and little else, and he exchanged it with his brother, who worked his opposite shift. Gregor rose, left the room and entered a standard Snowball residence. A circle, large enough for a central table, a couch facing the wall-screen, and, opposite the screen, the company-mandated machines ready and willing to exchange wages for company-approved food, drink, and de-sensitizing drugs that kept Snowball's residents from losing their minds.

Gregor did not see his mother or his father. The simulation could create bodies based on profiles, but Gregor refused to data-dump his parents into the program. This was a specific therapy, not a fond memory.

He left his childhood home through the rounded door, which trundled into its rightward slot like a slow, white-steel wheel. Beyond, Snowball's patchwork rock-and-metal construction blended natural comet with artificial reinforcements. The simulator never quite captured the comet's sheer cold, but Gregor didn't mind not wearing the thick clothing required anytime you ventured from the heated sections. The simulation gave that clothing, though, to everyone Gregor saw, the people now coming out to greet him.

Gregor wasn't a programmer, and he didn't take the time to tell some complex story. Every person here wore the same branded outfit, the same company logo patched onto their chest. While their faces differed through a million possibilities, all of them bore angry scowls, squinting eyes, and balled fists. Snowball's virtual residents wanted Gregor dead, and they attacked him with wild abandon. Gregor returned the same, crunching his violent way through Snowball's corridors with his fists, his hammer, and, on occasion, his head. Every impact felt real, every company soldier downed still fluttered his heart a little.

The simulator let Gregor play out a past he wished he'd lived, and Gregor reveled in it.

At the very end, the program began to deviate further

from reality. Gregor didn't have access to Snowball's blue-prints, didn't know every room, so as he fought further and further inside the company's offices, things became more variable, stranger. Rooms too large to exist in a comet's caverns appeared, as did equipment for industries Snowball could never support, like raising livestock or starship construction. The program picked them at random, and at first, Gregor would always stop here, kick himself back out. He'd since decided to regard the oddities as further evidence that the company had no idea what it was doing, that it was not only bad, but moronic.

The final room, with the endless pink-blue-purple nebula outside the window, held one person. A man nowhere near this high up the company's hierarchy, but, nonetheless, the one who'd forced Gregor off Snowball. Who'd stripped Gregor away from his family over a bar fight gone wrong. Of all the people in the simulation, Dawes was the only one Gregor had built. Impressions layered on one another to create the smarmy, awful bum that Gregor could get endless satisfaction destroying.

They faced off in a clear room, with only the nebula windows. Impractical for reality, perfect for fantasy. A thousand times Gregor had destroyed Dawes in this room, and this time would be no different. Dawes had no weapon —the simulator sometimes gave him one—so Gregor tossed aside his hammer to keep things fair.

Gregor went first, charging towards the smug grin, ready to lay Dawes flat with his big shoulder. Dawes, though, dodged to the side. Ran past Gregor's rush back to the room's entrance, to where Gregor had tossed the hammer. Dawes picked it up as Gregor turned around, and as Gregor tried to figure out what was going on—the simulator never played it this smart—Dawes ran at him, hammer held high. Gregor tried to step into, underneath

Dawes' swing, but the man seemed to know what Gregor would do and swung the hammer in a swoop from the side, catching Gregor in the ribs and sending him crashing to the floor. Before Gregor could react, Dawes stood over him, hammer ready. This time, Dawes didn't adjust his swing.

"Vengeance is a distraction," Aurora said when the simulator kicked Gregor out. She stood outside the machine, looking both bored and satisfied at the same time. "If you're going to keep running your little show, you're going to have to figure out how to beat him."

Gregor did, and then the next time Dawes hit harder, moved faster. Every time Gregor would beat Dawes, the next version would be tougher, and Gregor would spend more time in the simulator, pouring over it, until he learned. Dawes would always be there, ready and waiting, but Gregor chose to give him life. Chose to obsess.

Instead, he'd deleted the program. No more Dawes. No more distractions.

THIRTY-FOUR

Bad Deals

RACERS FLEW ON CONTRACTS. Deals drawn up to give them some payment assurance, some accident insurance before they sent their bodies careening across the stars. At the start, when Eponi had been sloughing her way through the trash troughs at the bottom, slamming skiffs for purses nowhere near her current DefenseCorp cash, the contracts had been simple one-pagers: a few lines declaring the sponsor not responsible for damages caused to Eponi's person or anything else. Sign here, collect cash, move on.

As Eponi flew her way to bigger and better leagues, with events that drew more than the drunks already at the race-course bar, the contracts magnified. They went for season lengths rather than a single race, promised whole outfits, crews, and transportation in exchange for Eponi's skills and willingness to get in front of the cameras as much as possible. Build the brand, the contracts said, and you will be rewarded. Once she'd done that, Eponi found herself getting called up to the head of her company, one stationed in the Sol system. Earth was right there, visible in the sky.

Not that Eponi set foot on it. She never had that kinda fame, that kinda cash.

Still, she'd sat across from someone infinitely more powerful and, on a galactic scale, more important than her and fought for a fair deal. She could negotiate. Not that the contract had saved her, in the end, but for a time it had been enough.

EPONI HAD FOUND her way down the level, made it near the room where Sai was busy hacking away at the creatures, and found the only entrance slathered in guards. All of them wore the head-to-toe suits Eponi had seen on all the Dynas guards, and having witnessed the diseases passing along those without, Eponi figured the whole cloth had less to do with enemy assaults and more with attacks of the bacterial variety. As to why some of the guards back at the base had been without the suits, like the one she'd kicked in through the window in the entry, Eponi couldn't say. Maybe they'd already been infected, maybe they just didn't care. Maybe the disease didn't get out that far.

Regardless, the simple path to saving Sai had been blocked. Eponi had already decided to save her friend, so pulling back now wasn't an option—racers had to stick to a path once it'd been committed, doubting led to crashes— but she couldn't exactly fight her way through a dozen guards either. Which meant a negotiation.

"Save him," Eponi said, loud and clear to the armed group watching Sai on screens next to the door. "Don't let him die."

One guard, bearing a blue triangle quartet on his shoulders, stepped in front of all the others at Eponi's words, stared down at her, and all Eponi could do was repeat her ask to those black-covered eyes and hidden face.

"What is he to you?" the guard replied.

"A friend."

The words prompted the other guards to draw their rifles, aim them at her, but the leader held up a single hand. Eponi flicked her eyes around, made sure none of the guards were about to shoot, and then continued.

"We were sent here to find someone. Our skiff crashed by accident."

Eponi wouldn't mention the dead guards, the others back at the base. Didn't seem smart.

"That's not a reason to save him," the guard replied. "That's a reason to kill him."

"What if we could help you?" Eponi replied. "We're not the only ones coming here."

"Talk, then."

"Not until you bring him in."

The guard stood still. No doubt running calculations through his head. Eponi could be telling the truth, in which case killing a good source of intel would be a terrible choice, or she could be lying, in which case they could just kill her later.

"You've got nothing to lose." Eponi nudged the guard a little. "I'm unarmed. He's not going to fight all of you."

Eponi wasn't sure about that one, but she had to try.

"You want us to save your friend?" the guard said. "Fine. Then you get him to come in here. We'll make sure he's taken care of, then you're going to say everything you know. If it's not very good, then we'll kill you right here."

"Deal."

Then they'd knocked Sai out. Eponi cursed them until one of the guards threatened to knock her out too, then she stopped, followed as they took Sai out of the room's antechamber. Every time Eponi tried to ask a question, tried to protest, one of the guards would tell her to shut it.

That didn't really stop her, but it didn't get Eponi any answers either.

When they came to the central lifts, the guards called two. The first one opened and, after shooing everyone inside it out, the guards dragged Sai inside. When Eponi started to join him, two other guards held her back. Let the doors shut, let Sai disappear.

"You're going to hold up your end of the deal," one of the guards said. "You're going up. Guess someone does want to hear what you have to say."

That someone, after guards led Eponi through a short lobby, past a desk-manning assistant who watched Eponi with zoo-like curiosity—an off-world specimen?—turned out to be another person in a white lab coat albeit one lined with gold triangles instead of blue or silver. The figure stood as Eponi walked into the hexagonal room, every side, except the one leading back to the lobby, a window instead of a wall. Dynas, daytime's white starlight slanting towards night, laid out for Eponi to see for a few kilometers until the view hit that mustard-yellow gas. Nothing clear beyond that.

The other guards with her backed off, slipped out of the room, leaving Eponi—still in her stolen uniform, if sans any gadgetry—alone with the new player.

"Can't say you have a great view from here," Eponi started. She'd ask about Sai in a hot second, but she wanted to get some idea of how this person operated. Had to learn the craft before you could fly it. "Dynas isn't a pretty planet."

The woman watched her. A central desk, overlaid with several monitors that split in the middle to show twin steel, featureless chairs, amounted to the only other features in the room. She didn't sit at her place, but instead paced back and forth at the room's far end, always keeping eyes on Eponi.

"Do you, uh, talk?" Eponi asked after several silent seconds. "Speak common?"

An absurd question, because nobody could command a city like this without speaking everyone's language, but what else was Eponi supposed to do? Stand there?

"I do talk," the woman replied, her voice a low, musical tone. "I also apologize, to you."

"Apologize?"

"Because you and your friends have been sent here to die."

"That's quite the statement."

The woman stared, or at least Eponi thought she did. She could be chatting through some transmitter with other people beyond the room. She could even be a decoy—Sever had seen that before, leaders who chose some chump to take the shots while they spoke from behind the curtain.

Eponi decided to take one of the seats, she'd been walking long enough.

Rather than sit down, Eponi slid the left chair so that it angled directly towards the right one, then sprawled herself out. Let her legs rest on the opposite chair, as if this conference was taking place on a beachside resort with margaritas instead of some doom tower's top on a damned world.

"What are you doing?" the woman said as Eponi completed her arrangement.

"You said we're going to die," Eponi replied. "Figured I might as well enjoy the moment."

"I . . . not immediately," the woman said. "Eventually. What we're doing here will—"

"I know. Diseases. You're all making a bunch of germs

for war or something. Don't care. What I want is my friend back, and a ship to get us off-world."

"You think you can make demands?"

Eponi leaned her head back, looked around the chair's edge towards the woman. "Definitely. Either you give me what I'm looking for, or when the rest of my friends arrive, all this goes boom. Your tower? Gone. City? Gone."

The woman laughed, but the sound came confused, a cover-up. "You would need an army."

"Ever hear of DefenseCorp? You hurt us, they'll come running in. Believe the phrase is 'nuke them from orbit'." Eponi held out her hand, inspected her nails. Scratched to hell after the skiff crash. "Either you give me what I'm asking for, or you're done. That simple."

Eponi had seen Aurora drop the DefenseCorp bomb before. Even if some random warlord or rebel figure thought they had one on Sever, the threat posed by DefenseCorp's inevitable revenge—DefenseCorp long held that letting anyone gain a victory over its forces would be bad for business, and retaliated against any aggression with extreme prejudice—tended to make the rage-monsters stop frothing at the mouth and mewl like a puppy.

This woman, though, didn't take the hint as was intended. She, instead, walked over to Eponi and looked down at her, hands loose at her sides.

"Nobody will come save you here, lost one," the woman said. "You're off the galactic edge, and the only thing left to do is fall."

THIRTY-FIVE

The Why

The tram coasted along without the slightest bumps, with a steady hum. The close tunnel walls provided a nothing view. Rovo watched the walls, watched Gregor staring out at those same walls, and watched Aurora watch them both. The tram's seats stayed against the sides, leaving the craft's middle open for, Rovo suspected, any heavier armor, vehicles, or equipment taking the ride.

"You keeping it together, rookie?" Aurora asked.

What a question. He'd nearly died several times over the past few hours, been chased through a base by hostile guards and nearly devoured by a hungry bacterial beast. But Rovo wasn't howling mad, wasn't spraying his rifle everywhere, or curling into a ball and crying, so . . .

"Yes?" Rovo tried.

"As break-in missions go, this one isn't the easiest," Aurora said. "Mine was a simple ship-to-ship assault. We took out a smuggling group. They had me kick the ones still alive out their own airlock."

"That's . . . brutal."

Aurora leaned forward, a movement that, in armor, involved so many parts shifting and clicking together that it sounded like Aurora had a thousand broken bones.

"DefenseCorp doesn't advertise that element," Aurora said. "They don't tell you that killing becomes a part of your daily life once you're in a squad like Sever. But they test you, even when you're not thinking about it. Everyone that gets in here, according to them, is a killer."

Rovo couldn't remember how many guards he'd shot with his rifle in the initial rush to the base, whether the two he'd knocked out in the office had died later. Blood might be on his hands already, but, like Aurora said, you had to be a killer to get into Sever. He wouldn't say he enjoyed the feeling, knowing he'd snuffed out lives, but, at least right now, it didn't weigh on him.

"Do you think I'm a killer?" Rovo asked Aurora.

"I think you're capable of it, which is what you need to be," Aurora said. "Whenever you hit the point where you're killing for fun, that's where things get dangerous. You ever risk the mission or the squad because you get too bloodthirsty, that's when you're done."

"Guess I'll watch out for that line." Rovo looked at his own hands, as if they could tell him where that line was, how close he was to flipping the homicidal maniac switch. He'd been close once, already. "I still don't get why we left Felix alive?"

"Because the mission takes priority," Aurora replied. "I wanted to take him out, after what he did, but part of being in this game is understanding why you play it."

"Why you play it?"

"Don't know about you, Rovo, but I'm not chasing monsters on faraway worlds for some noble cause. I want the cash so I can get out, get away from all this, and never have to do it again. We complete the mission, we get paid." Aurora stared forward, and while Rovo couldn't really make out her eyes through her visor, he thought she looked his way. "Why are you here, rookie?"

Rovo had reasons aplenty, but they all boiled down to one: boredom. That sounded too pathetic to say.

"I needed to prove I was worth more," Rovo said. "That I could do more than just fill out paperwork, pass along memos."

"Shooting randoms on Dynas is proof of that?"

"Not yet."

"Well, when you figure out what is, then you can decide if letting Felix live fits the why for you," Aurora said. "If it doesn't, and we're good on the mission, you can try to come back here, finish the job. Gregor might even go with you. He's got a soft spot for destroying things."

"You think we'll still win? The mission? Eponi and Sai are gone, and we don't even know where this thing's taking us."

"We're alive, Rovo. We've got our armor, most of our weapons, and an enemy that doesn't know we're coming," Aurora replied. "Hard to think of a better start. Sai and Eponi are either alive, and we'll rescue them if they are, or they aren't, and we'll make sure whoever killed them pays the price."

"Unless their killers are worth more to you kept alive."

"Right." Aurora didn't sound the least bit sad making that statement. "The why, Rovo. That's what matters most."

The why. Sure. Maybe Rovo would figure out a deeper one by the time he left Dynas.

If he left Dynas.

The why wouldn't matter much if he didn't.

. . .

READ *on for an excerpt from* HELIX STRIKE, *available free by signing up to my newsletter or at any retailer!*

An Excerpt from HELIX STRIKE

SEVER SQUAD BOOK TWO

Aurora snapped the bar in half, triggering a meltdown as she slipped the pieces into her mouth. A chocolate taste heaped with so many artificial elements ran across her tongue and down her throat, carrying all the effective nutrients, plus caffeine, that a battle-hardened soldier might need after waking up mid-mission.

Sever squad had been on Dynas for almost two days now, an adventure starting with a distress call from a planet supposedly inhabited by no one, but actually home to . . . what, Aurora still wasn't sure.

The five soldiers dispensed by DefenseCorp to handle the call had been given a clear objective: find the VIP who'd asked for the rescue, and no clear exit: find your own way off world with the objective in hand.

When Aurora had believed Dynas to be uninhabited, that arrangement didn't seem to make sense. Now that she, Gregor, and Rovo sat in an abandoned tram station beneath what felt, smelled, and sounded like a busy city, DefenseCorp's mission briefing felt like a lie.

Like every other galactic corporation, DefenseCorp

existed to make profits for its owners, employees, and various investors. How it stood to make money by sending Sever on a misguided, deceptive assault to nowhere wasn't clear to Aurora, but she knew how she'd get the answers: by shoving Admiral Deepak up against the wall and making him talk to her rifle's muzzle.

Rovo and Gregor didn't share her fervor. At least, not enough to wake them up on time. They'd each taken a bench on the tram as a bed, and Aurora had given them all five hours to rest. After a blood-soaked and blast-ridden first day, the dwindling adrenaline had left them all feeling hazy, unsure. Drained.

Aurora would be damned if she let her squad die due to exhaustion's ill effects.

Not that Aurora had all her squad. She'd left the squad's band open, set a message on repeat every few minutes asking for Eponi and Sai, the two missing members, to check in. If they had, Aurora's ear piece would've blasted her awake with an alarm.

Nothing had come, which meant Aurora snacked on the nutrient bar and watched the plastic blue-white light parade across the tram station in silence. Relative silence, anyway; above, she could hear engines rumbling, footfalls pounding, and distant shouts calling for this and that.

When Sever had arrived at the station, Aurora and Gregor had done a cursory look that found the station's sole entrance sealed by a locked gate, blocking not only their incoming platform but several others connecting to elsewhere in the city. Other maintenance options had been locked too, and while the tram's tunnel continued on, a flimsy metal barrier across the tunnel blaring CLOSED in red-painted letters echoed the surface door's sentiment: nobody would be coming this way.

The why wasn't too hard to figure. The first thing

Sever had found upon their arrival to Dynas had been an outpost overrun with strange half-human, half-fungal creatures. Felix, leading these things, had attempted to infect Sever squad. He'd failed, hard, and Aurora held to the idea that she'd be going back someday to finish that job. Genetic mutants like him were against Galactic law. More important, Felix had tried to hurt Sever, and people who attacked Aurora's squad didn't tend to live long.

Cash. Vengeance. Principles to live by.

Rovo sat up next. Aurora had taken last watch—the rookie had the middle, Gregor first. And while giving up those extra couple sleeping hours meant feeling even more sluggish, being tired beat being dead. Plenty of chemicals could help the former, nothing could help the latter.

The rookie didn't look too bad after his first day as a full Sever. Simulators could do wonders for training team tactics, for practicing your shots, but getting down on a grimy planet with a bunch of mercenaries loaded for combat stood apart from the screens and the goggles. Rovo had done well. Even gone off on his own for a bit, and while he'd followed Felix into a trap, that could be excused.

Like all rookies, he'd either learn, or he'd die early. Thus far, Aurora felt good about the kid. Not that she had many options if she didn't—Sever only had five members. You had to trust each one to do their jobs.

"No visitors?" Rovo offered as he wandered towards Aurora, sitting off of the tram and on the station's floor.

"Quiet, on all levels," Aurora replied, handing Rovo a protein bar.

Rovo crossed his legs, joined Aurora on the hard, dirty grey tile. His eyes tracked to the stairs heading up, behind Aurora and to his right. Wide enough, with a metal handrail splitting the steps, they seemed designed to handle a big crowd.

"Can't see anyone building a subway like this for a small outpost," Rovo said after he'd sucked down half the nutrient-loaded breakfast. "Has this entire mission been a big surprise, or is it just me?"

"Not you." Aurora nodded down the tunnel, where the tram could, if not for the barrier, keep going deeper into the city. "No way Dynas had the manpower and materials here naturally to make something like this. Whomever built this place had help, and that help came from off world."

"Which means DefenseCorp should have known about it."

"Deepak may not have, but I don't trust that," Aurora said. "So either we've been set up, or . . . "

Aurora and Deepak, the *Nautilus* commander and DefenseCorp admiral who'd sent Sever where they needed to go, didn't have what she'd call a good relationship. He stood fast by the need to play politics, to take top down orders and execute without questions. Aurora, well, Aurora didn't give a damn about authority until and unless obeying it meant the most cash in her account.

Even so, she had a hard time believing Deepak would send one of his best and most morally flexible squads on a pointless suicide mission. Where was the profit in that? If DefenseCorp just wanted to make a show of responding to the distress call, Deepak could've sent scrubs. Rounded up poor-performing recruits and sent them crashing to their swampy dooms in Dynas's depths.

"Or Deepak's hoping we can get out of this," Aurora said as Rovo munched away. "Either expose a secret, or destroy it."

"Sending five people to torch a city doesn't seem like a smart call," Rovo said. "Why not bring the *Nautilus* over and have it roast this place from orbit?"

"Too much noise," Gregor announced, roaming over

from the tram and brushing at bags under his eyes. "Blow up a planet, you have questions. Small team smashes the enemy? Subtle success."

"You're going to smash this whole place with that hammer?" Rovo asked.

"Might smash you," Gregor replied. "If you keep asking questions."

Aurora let them fall into their banter. Good to see the two had developed a bond, though that tended to happen fast on deadly missions. Saving each other's lives brought people closer.

Their armor suits, and Gregor's hammer, were back in the tram. They ought to go back there, squeeze them on and then go tramping up to the city, ready to spit fire and wreak havoc until they found Sai and Eponi. Except the sounds coming from above didn't seem all that menacing.

Walking over to the ramp and up it, Aurora went for another look at the chain gate sealing off the platforms. She felt Gregor and Rovo's eyes follow her, likely wondering what their commander was planning to do in her slim, mission-ready outfit. Meant to slip into the powerful suits, Sever didn't soar into combat wearing street clothes. Which would make her idea tricky.

Aurora didn't consider herself a stealth aficionado. She preferred the soldier to the spy, but charging out from here guns a-blazing would pit three mercenaries against what could be an entire city. Not exactly good odds.

"We need clothes," Aurora called back down, stopping her climb before she lost sight of the two others. "Ideas?"

"Clothes?" Gregor called back. "We have suits!"

"We're leaving them, at least for now," Aurora replied. "I'm not declaring war on this entire planet until we have to. Our mission is to get the VIP and get out."

"I thought we were doing pretty well," Rovo said.

"They sent a lot after us back at that outpost, but here we are?"

"We lost two people back there," Aurora said. "Against a couple skiffs worth of soldiers. We can't afford that again."

"And you think street clothes are going to—" Rovo stopped as Gregor put a hard hand on the rookie's shoulder.

"Question the commander? You do it up here," Gregor tapped his head with his other hand. "Not from your big mouth."

While Aurora wouldn't say Rovo looked thrilled at Gregor's advice, and Aurora herself didn't think blind obedience often worked as Sever's go-to commandment, she appreciated the big man's interruption all the same. Rovo didn't have the experience, and none of them had enough sleep, to question Aurora's decisions here.

Her plan, to get away from the tram station and get some idea about where they were, where Sai, Eponi, and the VIP might be, without drawing every gun in the city wouldn't have much success if they couldn't get outfits.

Once Aurora explained the idea, and once Gregor had finished his own breakfast, the trio fell in line. First they combed the tram station itself, looking for maintenance gear that might serve. Gregor's hammer served to break locks, but they found nothing: the supply closets only had some old tools and random gear designed to mark wet floors and wall off closed areas.

Which meant things would have to get messy.

Aurora, Gregor, and Rovo went up to the sealed gate leading to the street. Locked from the outside, the large gate blocked the entire staircase with its chain-and-metal bulk.

"Hammer?" Gregor said.

"Too loud," Aurora replied. "We're trying to be subtle here, not scare everyone."

"Much harder."

"Low power lasers ought to do it." Aurora poked at the spot on the gate where an unresponsive panel sat waiting to be woken up by someone with the proper clearance. "Carve right through this part and we'll be all right."

Gregor nodded, but Rovo had a funny look on his face. He stepped up to the door, with Aurora backing away to give the rookie room. Rovo inspected the panel, muttering to himself the whole time in a language Aurora didn't know.

"Rovo, what are you saying?" Gregor asked.

The rookie stopped, snapped his head up and had the good grace to blush a bit, "Sorry, I talk through things sometimes. My sisters used to tease me if I got things wrong when I did, so I learned not to do it in Common."

"You are a weird one." Gregor grinned. "But that is okay! We like weirdos."

"Rovo," Aurora interrupted. "The door? You have a better idea?"

"Uh, yeah, I think so. Back with my armor, I took a keycard off a guard back at the outpost. Looks like it might work here."

"And you're still standing there, why?"

Rovo's inspiration proved fruitful: he scanned the guard's keycard and the barrier blinked, then clicked itself loose. They could have peeled the whole thing away, but why invite just anyone down to look at their armor?

"Now, how do we get clothes?" Rovo said as they stood on the barrier's other side, looking out to fitful crowds wandering by in the early, yellow-skied morning.

"Bait," Gregor said, then looked towards Aurora. "Sorry, commander."

"Gregor, why should I be sorry?" Aurora relished the confusion on the big man's face. "It's your turn."

To leave the tram station, find their friends, and rescue the VIP, Sever squad couldn't go to war with an entire city. They'd need to stay undercover, and the best way to do that?

Send Gregor into the open, with no protection, to play the fool.

Continue the adventure with HELIX STRIKE, available free by signing up to my newsletter or at any retailer!

Acknowledgments and Author's Note

Sever Squad and its merry band of fortune-seeking soldiers came about as a counterpoint to some of my other fiction. These stories are more direct, more action-focused, a kind of letting off steam between longer, more complex works. I think of *Sever Squad* as the summer blockbusters to the fall Oscar fare: great fun and a good palate cleanser.

It's also a chance to spread my writing out a bit, to take on a slightly different genre and characters with a different background than I've done before. There's fun to be had in stretching the wings.

While this first book sets up Aurora & Co., you'll find the sequels round them out, expand their worlds in ways I certainly didn't plan when I started this series. I'm excited to see where they wind up, and hope you'll stick along for the ride.

As with any story, *Drop Zone* came to be because of the support from my family and friends, their unending willingness to push me forward. One of those friends, Joel, who you'll see dedicated in this book, walked with me to school in our kindergarten years. Our days spent adventuring through backyards and wooded hillsides in northern Wisconsin still ripple through the paragraphs I put together today.

I hope you'll enjoy the rest of *Sever Squad*, and I'll see you after the turn of the page.

About the Author

A.R. Knight spins stories in a frosty house in Madison, WI, primarily owned by a pair of cats. After getting sucked into the working grind in the economic crash of the 2008, he found himself spending boring meetings soaring through space and going on grand adventures.

Eventually, spending time with podcasting, screenplays, short stories and other novels, he found a story he could fall into and a cast of characters both entertaining and full of heart.

A.R. Knight plans on jumping through to other worlds and finding new stories to tell in the limitless borders of our imagination.

Thanks, as always, for reading!

For more information:
www.adamrknight.com

To Joel